nsew

short stories inspired by the Morningstar series

LJ FARROW

sustenance

yoshiwara district
tokyo, japan
1875

1

THE COLLECTOR MADE HIS WAY through the deepening dusk, seeking means of sustenance, and undertaking other critical errands for his mistress. Tokyo's taverns were beginning to fill as people made their way home from the factories. At night, Yoshiwara came alive, its denizens doing a brisk business in secret trades and criminal alliances, and the flesh peddlers here were legendary.

Although he had never officially been a samurai, he still felt keenly the absence of the swords at his waist. Such as these had been a reminder to those others who would interfere with him; although his appearance still betrayed him as other, the weapons were a subtle sign of station, signaling that he had a master. The steel had given those who would otherwise readily abuse him pause, its protection he now lacked following the concession of Yoshinobu, Azuma's kinsman, the fifteenth Shogun of the Tokugawa line.

Following the Meiji Restoration, feudal law had been swiftly outlawed by Imperial edict, and samurai were no longer allowed to go about publicly wearing their weapons; their honored status had been stripped from them. He smiled bitterly. Swords or no, those who interfered with him regretted such actions uniformly.

Lanterns were more widely spaced along these thoroughfares, likely purposefully, to allow the many clandestine assignations that occurred here to play out under cover of darkness. He was mindful of the fact that such conditions also favored brigands, and his dress signaled him part of a noble household, a potential target for thieves.

He had once made a point of disguising himself in peasant dress, in those days when he could return insults readily at the point of a blade, but he found that now, it was his clothing that made others wonder at his position before willingly lashing out at his foreign countenance. Besides, he had no need to hide, he was amply equipped to defend himself.

There was one exception to the gloom. Along the central boulevard of the district, lanterns blazed forth, illuminating storefronts that had been converted to enormous, latticed cages. Beyond the stout slats of each of these establishments huddled nearly a hundred young women. This display was purposeful, and had the same goal as any merchant who plied wares. Their bodies were for sale. A potential customer from the common classes could have his pick of these unfortunates; it was what had become of the *kabuki* and the *geisha* from a more civilized time. A time that the Collector suspected was now lost.

A more affluent visitor could be received in the attached brothel, where the youngest and prettiest had been curated for those who could afford to be discerning. His mistress had occasionally taken to intervening on behalf of such unfortunates as inhabited the storefront.

From the far corner of the cage, his attention was drawn to one whose appearance was so unlike that of her sisters that he was surprised she was on display. The proprietors did all they could to mask those who were less fair of face, or malnourished, or frankly diseased with all manner of silken clothing and cosmetics, artifice that was stripped from these women at dawn, when they were relegated to other menial duties of the household. Some were obviously high, drugged into submission, or perhaps were maintained in a habit that allowed them to be controlled.

This one had the barest costuming, wearing only a reasonably beautiful midnight blue kimono without adornment, in the fashion of a farmgirl. It was well-worn, and despite its shabbiness, its owner had a stubborn attractiveness, though she resisted the prodding of the brothel's matron to smile and pose. Most striking of all was her shorn hair, bluntly cut short, artless and defiant, likely something she had done to herself in protest of her station. Despite these shortcomings, she put to shame those others with whom she shared this prison. Indeed, she had the bearing of one who could not be caged, could not be owned, could not be controlled in spite of her indenture.

The matron's shrewd eye noticed the Collector's interest, and sized up his fine clothing, and in a simpering voice she appealed to him. "Ah, she is young but forgotten. Headstrong. No one. You could treat her as you wish, although she often needs reminders of what is expected of her." She signaled to one of her assistants, a young man with a cudgel, who stood inside the cage and waded across toward the girl with a menacing expression that did not bother to hide his pleasure at the prospect of making her submit. "Come forward, girl. This *gentleman* has shown you favor." The emphasis and the irony in her voice transmitted her notice that he was not Japanese. Perhaps that was why she encouraged him in his interest. Matchmaking in her way, putting nothing with nothing.

When the young woman set her face in a resolute scowl and did not respond, the bully boy approached her aggressively, more than happy to trade violence for obedience.

"If you beat her, I will take my money elsewhere," the Collector said, and the matron missed the underlying warning in his tone.

"Foreigner, I can call my husband and his associates, and have *you* beaten. You are not master here," she protested, feigning boredom, thinking her position a secure place from which to make such a threat. Most of these establishments were either run or owned by powerful crime lords with access to a vast criminal network.

"Then you would find yourself soon without a husband, without protection. Foolish woman, you should seek no quarrel with me," he told her, and this time she saw that thing in his eyes that told her all she needed to know, and he was satisfied when she turned her own gaze downward, away from what she witnessed in his.

"My apologies," she rushed to say, in a vastly different tone of voice. When she continued, she had regained her composure, and was much more deferent. "Speak with her if you will, it is nothing to me. Perhaps you can coax her without force; she seems to require a strong hand." She turned slightly away, to deal with other customers who awaited her attentions, freeing him to approach the cage.

He gave an abbreviated bow of respect in the girl's direction. She was noticeably young, probably having attained no more than fourteen or fifteen years of age, and he was reminded of those early years with Azuma, and Megumi, who had also been heartbreakingly young once, although their fortunes quite different than this creature's. He was inured to the ridicule that this engendered among the other women in the cage, they tittered at this waste of honor on the lowest of their own and turned away from him in subtle insult. He was used to disdain, and ignored them.

This garnered her attention in a new way. She was unused to respect, though he suspected he knew something of her from her revolutionary haircut. She had earned the dislike of these women, but it was for something she believed in, and it was likely she would have advocated for them in their shared plight, given an opportunity. They were all too foolish to understand.

She approached the bars warily. Her eyes blazed with intelligence, and many questions that he was certain she would never voice. Her expression betrayed no evidence of distaste at his countenance. When finally she stood before him, he felt her unnatural warmth across the abbreviated distance between them. Heat radiated from her in waves, the throes of an unrelenting fever. One she was accustomed to, and he was saddened. This one would soon die, perhaps not last another year. She was riddled with consumption.

She refused to bow to him, another slight for which she could be beaten, but he ignored this. It pleased him, her turning away from meaningless duties and empty expressions of gratitude. For what? A lover unwanted and unasked for?

"I am urgently expected elsewhere," he told her. "But if I am not too…repugnant to you, I would like to return tomorrow and call upon you for companionship. I think you would not find me so distasteful as some other men."

Her eyes betrayed surprise for only an instant before she remembered herself and resumed her practiced indifference. He was pleased. She was emotionally strong, this one.

"Come now, sir." The matron's voice called down to him. "I must insist you move on; these girls are not here to provide conversation. I have a business to run." These statements she managed in a tone of compliant suggestion, in an attempt to avoid offense or elicit retaliation of the sort he had hinted at earlier.

In response, the Collector handed her a goodly sum of crisp new *yen*, with his instructions. "I will return tomorrow. You will receive this sum again when I confirm that my wishes have been met. She is to be removed from this cage and bathed. If I find she has been abused, or used for the pleasures of another man, there will be consequences." He appealed to her greed but was not above the threat, which he felt she needed. Some personalities respond better to hardship than to reward, and he knew the matron was one of these. "There is no need to adorn her in anything other than what she wears now. Tell me, what is her name?"

"Her?!" The matron scoffed, but the money disappeared as if she were performing a magic trick. "She will not tell us any other than Nōnēmu."

The Collector threw back his head and laughed, startling the matron so much that she inadvertently took a step back. Often, his laughter was what marked him as a monster. He *was* amused, but if the matron was also frightened at the incongruity of his mirth, so be it. His orders would be followed. His amusement came from the knowledge that these women often lied about their names, most of them choosing something they felt would be attractive, or pleasing, to the men they served. The most common name they assumed these days was Haruko, the name of Prince Meiji's bride, as it was currently popular. This extraordinary child had told the matron she had 'no name.'

2

HE RETURNED LATE TO THE sprawling residence in the hills of Yamanote that he shared with his mistress and the *Akai*, skirting the grounds of the Imperial Palace on his way up to the heights. The Great Fuji-san was a spectre in the distant darkness. The weather remained warm on these late spring evenings, though it would cool overnight, shrouding the hills in a fine mist and painting the grass with sparkling dew.

The cherry trees beyond the gate were still in full flower, and he paused beneath their canopies, enjoying the fragrance as he did each year. Soon his beloved butterflies would return to adorn the expansive gardens.

His mistress sought him in the depths of the night, when she returned from her own forays, to receive his reports of his doings in the city. In due course, they discussed crucial plans, strategies of engagement for ongoing business and political interests. Though he thought to tell Azuma of the girl he had encountered, something stayed this urge, and he kept this from her for now.

"You are distracted tonight, my friend," she observed astutely that his thoughts were elsewhere, and he immediately apologized for his inattentiveness, but she turned away the apology, scrutinizing him carefully. "I had thought you would feed, but you have not."

"I put it off to address other more essential concerns," he told her dismissively, in a ploy to deflect her shrewd scrutiny. She knew him wholly, as they were bound by the dark gift of her power, and if she generally did not intrude on his intrigues, he knew all too well that she could compel him to share his blood, and then he could hide nothing. "I will attend to those wants tomorrow. I am concerned about ensuring that your guard are fully numbered."

He felt that this consideration would distract her from any of his strange behavior. *Jūichi* had failed his mistress and was the latest embarrassment to be added to the Collector's butterfly garden. This mythical place was referred to with reverence and awe, even fear, by the fiercest of the *Akai*, none of which desired to be retired there. But longevity conferred madness in some, and *Jūichi* had betrayed his oath, and endangered the Dragon Goddess with his foolish mutinies. Thus *Jūni* had ascended in number and was advanced, and the sacred guard was deficient by one.

"Yet this is not what distracts your thoughts," Azuma remarked archly, but with a smile that told him he was safe from further probing. He was surprised at his relief. They two were not keepers of secrets from one another, but something in him stubbornly wanted to safeguard the story of the girl for himself for now. It was a selfishness unusual to him, and he had to face the idea that some vulnerable part of him had been touched by the young unfortunate. Possibly this was the reason for his reticence; Azuma had a legendary soft spot for disenfranchised young women, and he was perhaps afraid that she would be overly interested in this one. His latent jealousy both bewildered and amused him; he and the Dragon had never competed for the affection of any human. She would, perhaps, not fully understand his ardor, but would respect the boundaries of his desires.

She had never interfered with any of his consorts, although over the centuries it had become clear that their preferences in a companion were usually singularly different.

3

HE WAS GREETED WITH FALSE anticipation, if not respect, on his return to the establishment in Yoshiwara the following evening. The matron raised her eyebrows meaningfully as she counted his second payment, and made bold to suggest that such a distinguished gentleman might be better served in the upper rooms of the brothel. "Surely our finest would suit your tastes better?" she offered, and he understood her greed. She was moved by the amount of money he carried, and he could not blame her for trying to get more of it. She was probably as much prisoner here as the women she herded and cultivated like cattle, subject to the whims of husband, brother, even son. Shades of grey.

"So bring my chosen into the house, and we shall want tea," he nodded curtly, handing over an additional sum with an expression that told her it was his final payment.

"*We?!*" The woman laughed shrilly with false delight. "My, how fancy a gentleman we have," she remarked, glancing at him from under her lashes in an attempt to disguise her disdain.

He respected her consistency of personality; he understood that she found the girl and himself to be beneath even her contempt, but his money spent the same as any other. If nothing else, it was a language he could easily use to communicate with her and those like her. Yet he could see she found him tiresome in a way, because she could not easily manipulate him.

The proprietress nodded curtly to another of the young men in the hallway, and the Collector was ushered to an elegant parlor on the second floor. The tapestries and bedclothes were of silk, moderately good quality, and recently laundered. The windows overlooked the street, but the louvered shutters had been pulled to, in order to diminish the sounds of the busy thoroughfare and the brisk business taking place below stairs.

He lowered himself slowly and kneeled on the fragrant tatami mat near the window, and undertook his prayers while he waited. Some little time later, he heard the minor scuffle in the hallway and smiled. She made nothing simple for them. It sounded as though she had resisted the boy enough that he was forced to drag her along the gallery, but there were no sounds of violence, so he knew his warnings against beating her had been heeded.

He did not turn when the door was opened, simply waited for her captor to propel her into the room and depart. The door was firmly closed, and he paused a few moments more before turning around.

The first thing his heightened senses could ascertain in the dim candlelight had nothing to do with her appearance. Rather it was the furnace of her body heat that he could feel on his exposed skin, like the banked embers of a dying fire. Closer inspection confirmed that she was slighter of build than one would expect, because she was unfortunately fueling the blaze with her sickness, feeding her flesh to the disease that raged within her.

She was certainly lovely despite her lack of ornamentation. She wore the same simple kimono, and her hair was perhaps even more unruly following her bath. Her eyes were large and luminous, and finally showed a touch of fear. Although perhaps it was uncertainty, since it was clear she had never been brought to these rooms before, and it made her mistrustful. She had learned enough of the world to know that greater riches and power did not necessarily increase civility but could rather encourage or condone a largesse of cruelties.

She scanned the room carefully, taking particular note of the position of the windows and very subtly reexamining the door she had just come through. The Collector was delighted, as he recognized her taking note of modes of escape. In spite of all he knew of her, she had not abandoned hope.

Once again, he bowed to her, but she again refused to return this courtesy, and he could see her distrust.

"The mistress tells me that you have no name," he remarked kindly, expecting no response. He got none.

Her posture was straight, formal even, and he approached her. She was taller than average, but her illness was already trying to engender infirmity, and he suspected that her fragility made her angry. He sensed her impatience with the situation, and was amused by it, but did not remark upon it.

The tea arrived, and he surprised her again by serving her, before retreating to the window once more with his own cup. He could see her suspicion now.

Finally, she spoke, in a voice heavy with agitation that she did not bother to disguise. "Why delay the inevitable? You are not here to court me."

These words could earn her a beating, and she knew this, but she was tired of artifice, if ever she had tolerated it.

"Am I not?" he challenged her, and for this statement he was rewarded with a response. The slightest tilt of her head, her fine features concentrating on this, the unexpected. It was subtle but he did not miss it; she was unable to hide her interest in his tone.

"When they bathe us, I know some noble has requested it, out of fear of catching some disease and taking it home to his wife," she responded bitterly. Ah. It was ghastly for them if special preparations were made; the treatment that came after was often worse than what they were subjected to in their everyday routine. He understood her perfectly.

"Yet the disease you have cannot be cleansed away with soap," he observed quietly, and he registered the astonishment in her eyes before she looked away from him.

"No," she said quietly, relaxing enough to sit on the floor and take up the teacup. "And you are not safe from it, or me, in this room."

"But your cough has gone," the Collector observed with some wisdom.

"It has, but perhaps only because there is not enough of me left to sustain it," she replied sadly, and he saw that she was aware of the deadly course of her illness; in some, near the end, their lungs had not the strength to cough. And now, sitting together in the silence, he could hear that her breaths came more rapidly than one would expect of such youth, the flutterings a polite whisper, like the rustling of a bird's wings. And then, because he felt that she could not master her natural curiosity about the course of their conversation, she asked, looking down at her tea, "Why did you serve me?"

"Look upon me. You may believe that you have no station, but you possess more than I. You are, at least, to be counted among the Japanese. Your consent to my presence is a kindness; you could refuse to share your tea with me as an affront to your honor. Even your matron recognizes this."

"Consent suggests I could refuse you," she remarked quietly.

"And so you could," he assured her. "It would be unlawful to force a daughter of the Rising Sun to lie with a foreigner against her will. That prohibition is still clearly supported in this society."

"Even if not in this establishment," she replied sourly. "But you waste your time. Whether or not you fear the contagion, if you are going to use me, I prefer that you proceed as you appear to ignore the risk."

"I am not susceptible to this affliction, not as you might think," he told her.

But she was not reassured by this, saying bitterly, "Your wealth will not protect you, nor your youth. The consumption is indiscriminate in its reach."

"I have nothing to fear from you," he told her sadly, realizing the lie as it passed his lips. If she were to reject him, his foolish heart would yet sustain an injury.

"Then get on with it," she sighed, moving to loosen her kimono, but he came to her and stayed her hands.

"What I desire from you is not your flesh," he assured her, and placed gentle hands on her shoulders when he sensed the spike in her fear.

"Do you not do as other men?" she asked him, searching his face in curious inquiry, because she realized there was nothing there to terrify. She was too young to realize that he was more dangerous than any of the men she had encountered here, or perhaps she saw what he meant her to, that he would not harm her.

"If you wonder whether I partake of congress with women, I have that capacity, I admit to those desires. And you would be a gift for such as I, but I have another need, one of greater immediacy."

She hesitated for the first time. "Are you going to hurt me?" Her question held neither fear nor resignation.

"It is not what you expect, and I hope that you will take pleasure of it," he told her honestly, but still she held herself apart, understandably unsure.

"Perhaps you find me repulsive?" he asked her without censure. "What I want from you resides in the life you still own, in your blood, and I ask you this question because what I propose is far more intimate than sex."

"You may take of me what you need," she assented quietly, adding honestly, and somewhat shyly, as if her admission surprised even herself, "I would not mind the other."

This inflamed him all the more, and he took her in his arms, gifting her with pleasure before he allowed himself to feed. And her blood told him more than he had guessed at, and it saddened him as much as it satisfied his thirst.

4

HE STILL COULD NOT BRING himself to unburden his discovery to his mistress, and if Azuma noticed this odd preoccupation, she did not mention it. They continued their plans to replace *Jūni*, but neither discussions on the subject nor the vetting of candidates from the Sect were fruitful. The Collector was pleased that the Dragon had shown no favor to any of the possible replacements that had been put forward, but the asymmetry of her protective detail bothered him, particularly in this still uncertain time, when Imperial Rule was not indisputably established. Its fragility worried him.

There were still samurai in hiding in the southern provinces that had failed to surrender fealty to the Emperor, and they were a threat to the enduring peace. Azuma accepted that her descendant cousins had not maintained the strength of the shogunate, and she embraced the change that had accompanied Imperial restoration.

She held her power as a member of the Mashaito clan, as the industrial ruling class had ascended in favor. She styled herself as a young widow who had inherited her deceased husband's riches in the absence of any *living* male relatives, or children of her own. Thus she maintained an untouchable place in society.

Those who would challenge her refused to do so, believing a woman to be an insignificant threat. They might admit to some apprehension about her bondsman, clearly a child of misfortune, but if they questioned the Collector's inclusion in her household, she was otherwise beyond reproach. And her security detail seemed to protect her interests with religious fervor. She remained sought after as a consort as much for her beauty as her riches, but it was whispered that she disdained the company of men, indeed it was rumored that she and her mythical husband had lived separate lives.

Under such pretenses, Azuma pursued those amusements that entertained her interests. She was afforded a life of leisure, but she continued her study of illness, politics, and stories of the supernatural. Akenomyosei was a regular visitor to the estate in Yamanote, but it appeared that the monster and his protégé did little more than exchange banter and gamble. The Collector kept his distance.

And between his mistress and himself, they contained, corralled, cajoled, and tolerated Tatsuo Tomo in his unexpected emergences. This unfortunate reality largely kept them from public life, and Azuma rarely appeared at court to minimize any confusion it might cause or to circumvent dishonor that could be laid upon the household.

When finally he approached her about this most unexpected and unusual of prospects, she listened with interest, and sympathy, but no real approval that he could discern.

"She cannot be otherwise saved, and you care for her," Azuma observed astutely, seeing through to his underlying feelings. "But this life is not for everyone, certainly not for just anyone. And while I admire her spirit, defiance does not make a good canvas for the art of devoted service."

"Promise me you won't dismiss the idea out of hand, *Aijin*," he appealed, kneeling before her as he had not done since that long-ago day in the Shogun's library. He addressed her formally both to punctuate his sincerity and signal his fealty. He wanted to reassure her that he would not pit his will against hers.

"I trust your assessment, my dear friend. You have taught me much. Yet I have rarely seen this much emotion from you, who are dispassionate as a matter of necessity. Think hard on this, as your recommendation carries much weight with me. There are many difficult tests that must be faced on the road to becoming a priest of the Crimson Guard."

5

HE WAS CALLED AWAY FOR a time, sent by the Mistress to attempt to reason with the rebels in the south. These fruitless endeavors ended with a violence that he had received permission to deploy in the event that diplomacy failed, an unavoidable alternative, and he was reminded of the futility of Ryukyu, centuries before.

These attentions ate months of his time, rather than weeks, and on his return, while he was grateful to be coming home, his thoughts were distracted by concerned imaginings that he would arrive too late, that his charge in Yoshiwara would be gone. Not for the first time he cursed himself for not buying her freedom outright, and installing her as his consort at Yamanote, but the *Akai* had only one context for him, and he needed to maintain it. He also knew that the dangers she faced from the *harimise* were slightly less than those she might encounter in Azuma's household. In moments of complete honesty he also had to admit that he was too jealous when faced with the possibility that she could choose Azuma over himself.

He turned his horse toward the city, stabling the animal a few blocks outside the central district and continuing on foot to the now familiar brothel. The matron took his money without speaking, signaling to her assistant to escort him. She nodded knowingly, as if the niceties of any exchange were no longer necessary; he was hooked, and she owned his drug of choice. It should have made him angry, but his concerns lay elsewhere.

They dared present her to him with signs of violence, some old and some new. He viewed the bruises around her eyes, the crust on her split lip, with the barest remove. His fury could not be denied, and he cursed them for their stupidity. Did they not know that for her he would tear the building down and leave none standing to reverse this insult? They could not know the depth of his ire, that retribution was his stock in trade.

But her posture suggested that she believed what she saw in his eyes was directed at her, so he banked this outrage and kneeled at her feet, pulling her down to him, stroking her hair gently as she wept, whispering to him that they had beaten her because she would not report on him, would not address their desire to solve the mystery of his riches, refused to lessen the intrigue of this exotic being. It was true then, these criminals used their prostitutes blatantly, as spies, hoping to elicit information that would give them some sort of political leverage, some fodder for blackmail.

She had borne these insults and refused to betray him. Perhaps here was something to offer to Azuma that she would value. Loyalty.

And the young woman clung to him in relief that he had returned, but she worried about the state of his person. She was awed by the homicidal rage that lived in every line of his posture, and he felt her fear. So to calm her, he lied, "I still do not know your name. I want to hear your story. I want to know of your life." This was purposeful, as her nearness and this new kind of intimacy had the power to calm him, despite what her blood had already revealed.

He was afraid she would refuse this, as it required her to expose herself even more than she already had. But she relented, and her soft voice was a balm to his outrage. As she spoke of her childhood in Yeso, he mastered his surprise, as it had coincidentally been the provenance of the Lady Megumi. She told him of her father, a simple farmer who had suffered a bruised honor when his daughter refused the offer of a more powerful landowner, and in retaliation had sold her to a textile industrialist.

The working conditions had been so poor that she and many another young woman had become ill, and the tuberculosis that stalked them in those quarters had been relentless and uniformly deadly. But death was a mercy to the suffering of the factory, the endless hours, the inadequate provisions, the sanctioned abuses, where the male supervisors took great pleasure in harassments and predatory attacks that none of the women had any recourse to address.

In her case, her father had washed his hands of her, she was far from home, and already had symptoms of the sickness. In protest, she had cut off all of her hair in an attempt to decrease her attractiveness to them, to defeminize herself, and they ridiculed her mercilessly but did not cease their torments. Finally, coughing up blood, she had collapsed on the factory floor, and they had sold her to the brothel. Men came and dragged her the entire distance from the factory to the central district of Yoshiwara, leaving her in the cage to live or die, to be used up of any part of her that was left, reduced to less than nothing.

"Yet you never believed them. You never forgot you are someone," the Collector observed quietly, as she leaned against him.

"Not anymore," she smiled, pulling away, freeing herself from his embrace. The kindness in it brought her pain, as she knew it to be a transitory part of her existence. "I am almost gone, and where I am going, they can no longer reach me, no longer compel me to do anything."

"What if there were another choice?" he asked her.

"There is no other choice," she said softly, thinking that her tone would soften the blow, force him to relinquish the denial she believed he suffered on her behalf.

"I could offer you freedom," he asserted, "and power." She could hear that he was in earnest; he believed what he said.

"You are a foreigner," she pointed out, shaking her head as though she knew something he did not. "No matter that it appears that you are in the employ of a powerful Master, surely your Lord would not uphold your word as his own."

"My patron is a woman. My mistress knows of you, and you could join me in my service to her," he told her, pleased at her surprise to learn he gave his loyalty to another of her sex.

"And trade one collar for another?" She shook her head. "Why should anyone purchase my bond? My death is certain."

"That you reach for death without fear is what sets you apart; it is a part of that which gives you worth to me. The question is whether you can yet remember your worth to yourself. If you can, there may still be more for you to do in this life, in a manner which will restore your status as a person." The Collector stressed this last point, because it was the only thing that anyone could now offer her that had any value.

"So you propose to free me from this place?" she asked. Her lips twisted with bitterness and irony because she knew that the matron would refuse any offer from someone that might care for her. That the woman would make such a decision out of an abundance of jealousy and mean-spiritedness, eager to ruin any chance at another's happiness. They would beat her to death rather than release her.

"No." The word had such finality to it that she wanted to despair. But then he continued, recognizing that there was something he could do for her to help her see that she did indeed have choices. It was essential to let her do something for herself.

"You must free yourself from your own prison." He paused, and held up a finger in warning at what he read in her eyes, understanding what she wanted to do, and how she wanted to do it. "But you must accomplish this without bloodshed. It is this currency that will buy your admission to the Mistress' household. You will pay an even greater price to be found acceptable to remain in her service. I must take my leave of you now, and I shall not return. Find me in the garden of the house at the top of Yamanote after dark in three days' time. I will remain there until the first rays of dawn strike the face of Fuji-san. Do not fail me in this, or we shall have to resume our discussions in the next life."

And with this pragmatic concession to Azuma's warnings, he took leave of her, refusing to tarry any longer or to look back.

6

SHE ARRIVED AUSPICIOUSLY AT THE birth of a new day, at the midpoint of the night, a perfect time to begin a new life. And because she did not at first see him there, under the trees, when he came up behind her and touched her arm, she raised the cudgel that she had stolen from her tormentors, ready to fight for what little life she had left.

"She just might do, my friend," Azuma's voice startled them both from the nearby garden. The Collector smiled to himself, assured that this unusual expression of his feelings could not be discerned in the darkness.

As he had guessed she would, she successfully assumed the mantle of responsibility expected of the *Akai*, and adapted to becoming one of the numbered with remarkable aplomb.

Over the years, she kept a diary of sorts, a ledger, an accounting of names and dates. It marked the occasion of the deaths of every occupant of her former places of sorrow. Like his butterflies, he recognized it as her particular collection. She put it aside once she had survived them all, leaving the past where it rightly belonged.

And if she were shown favor among her fellow priests, it was because she earned it, and she rose steadily through the ranks of the *Akai*. Within a century she had ascended among their number and was called *Ni*.

deliverance

oltepesi
rift valley, kenya
1632

1

"ENKAI SAVE YOU IF I catch you underfoot again!" Chiumbo's mother, Nyere, scolded him sharply but could not keep a stern face and ended up laughing. She rubbed his tight curls affectionately, and shooed him from the hut.

The old women in the village said his mother was plain, which his grandfather suggested was a nicer way to say that she was ugly. Grandfather was *Ama*'s father.

Chiumbo thought that Grandfather was teasing, but he could not know. He wrinkled his face as he peered back in at her, watching while she darted in and out of their dwelling to attend her cooking fire. He loved the pink brightness of her headcloth, liked to trace the pretty little scars that dotted her cheekbones, and watch the sunlight reflect off of her dangling earrings.

He had wondered and wondered why he could not find anything wrong with her. He worried about his eyesight, until one day, fishing with Gatimu, his father, on the Olololong'a River, Father had told him a Great Secret. One that he said the old women did not know.

Father said that Nyere was the most beautiful creature *in the world*. Chiumbo was amazed.

"*Aba*, how do you know this?" he queried.

"Because I have been from the Great Lake to the Eastern Coast, and I have yet to find another with such great beauty," Father concluded.

"Outside the Great Valley?"

"Oh, yes, and Beyond," Father said this with gravity, as though the observation was a weighty thing in its own right.

"Well, I think so, too," Chiumbo said, in a self-congratulatory tone. "But I do not know why it is a Great Secret."

"Well, there is a magic that you use on your eyes, and the old women in the village do not know this magic despite their many years."

"And *Ama*'s father has no magic then, either." Chiumbo pointed this out. "He explained-"

"Chilemba has plenty of magic," Gatimu replied with a chuckle. "He was pulling on your big toe. He wants you to think for yourself. He knows his daughter is no ugly woman."

Chiumbo was relieved to hear this. But then despairing again, when he thought about what Father had told him.

"What is it, my son?" Gatimu asked, without even looking away from the river. Chiumbo always wondered how Father knew what he was thinking, and he suspected this was another magic, like the one Nyere used on him to find him when he was trying to avoid taking a bath.

"*Aba*, I do not know how to use the eye magic," Chiumbo explained.

"It is simple, but you must keep the secret and only share it with those who understand such things," Gatimu warned.

"How will I know who they are?" Chiumbo wondered aloud.

"You will just know, and you will know how you will know, when you need to know it," Father assured him, but Chiumbo was too impatient to know the secret of the magic to try to unravel this riddle now.

Father then pulled his net out of the river, and handed several fish to Chiumbo to carry to shore.

Chiumbo did so quickly, scrambling back down the bank and into the water, forgetting not to splash, which earned him a frown from Father.

"You are frightening our dinner."

"Sorry, *Aba*. You were telling me about the eye magic?" Chiumbo prompted again.

"Well," Father began, but then narrowed his eyes carefully at his son, as if deciding whether to part with what he knew. Chiumbo tried to be patient; he saw the sparkle in Gatimu's eyes that meant he was teasing.

"First, you must squint until all you can see is your own eyelashes," Gatimu demonstrated, and the boy mimicked him. "Then, you must quietly – this is the important part for you, my son – with no talking," Father opened one eye to see that Chiumbo was listening before he continued, "concentrate on what you are looking at."

"But I cannot see!" The boy protested.

"Aach. No talking. The magic only works when you are observing in silence," Gatimu admonished him. "Then you must listen, and the magic will tell you what is truly in front of you, the essence of it, and you will see what is important. Your heart will overcome your sight, so that you may no longer be fooled by your vision. That is how you will know that it is working."

Chiumbo thought he understood, but he imagined that it was something he would have to practice in order to master such magic. He was honored that Father had told him the Great Secret.

2

CHIUMBO WALKED BACKWARD FROM THE hut, and he realized that he must have had some natural magic of his own, because he did not have to squint to see his mother clearly.

Ama was pregnant, and in the heat she was impatient with him. She was far more exhausted than she used to be when she returned from collecting water. He wanted her cuddles still, as he always had, and she held him in the evenings, but the baby was pushing him farther away with each moon. Chiumbo was excited to see a little baby, a baby that belonged to *Ama* and *Aba* the same way he did. A baby that would also belong to Chiumbo, Father had told him.

He crossed the expanse of the central village, kicking up puffs of red clay dust as he went along. He understood how the sun could make one disagreeable, when it was so hot, and though he had worked up a rhythm with his kicks, he stopped when the rooster crossed his path.

It spoke out its protest, and Chiumbo could not help but look at its feet, scaly, a bit scary. He wondered if the village *mganga* would add those feet to his collection when the animal was harvested, and he shivered despite the shimmering heat.

He sped up, then, scurrying past the edge of the village that met a stand of trees that marked the path to the *mganga*'s hut, which had been set back among the shadows. There was a small fence made of sticks and mud, and this was adorned with the bones of many animals. Beads and shells were strung from the trees, and the clearing had a smell that was neither pleasant nor unpleasant. On the rare occasion that he was ill, the mganga had sometimes come to see him, and he was relieved that there was never a reason that he had to enter that place.

He refused to run, though he wanted to, every time he had to pass by it. He shivered, thinking about the old medicine man, sure that no amount of eye magic would improve that odd, fierce countenance.

He found Grandfather awake in his hut, working on something. He nodded in acknowledgement when he sensed his grandson had arrived, putting aside whatever he was working on to greet him.

"What have you brought to me today?" Grandfather inquired with a toothless smile.

"Just a stone, for the garden," Chiumbo replied. "You already know this, Grandfather."

"Well, perhaps I am not too old to be surprised one day," the elderly man told him, turning his attention to the offering his grandson carried. "White again?"

"Yes. I search the streambed, and each day I think I will find another color, but these are pretty, and I always choose the one that calls to me. The white ones have the loudest voices."

"Understandable," Grandfather allowed. He swept his arm toward the space just outside the door where they had been collecting the stones, one for each day of Nyere's pregnancy. It was a way to keep Chiumbo occupied, and allow him some form of participation during the long wait. He added the new stone to the outermost arm of the spiral he had been constructing. It was getting big, enough stones in the pattern to reach the length of his outstretched arms.

It must be close now, he thought, remembering what *Aba* and *Ama* had told him about the baby, how he himself had grown inside his mother through the hard rains, and the light showers, and the green mists, until his birth at the height of the dry season.

"So long!" he had protested when he heard of it. "I will run out of stones!" This had made them all laugh, although Chiumbo had no idea why his statement was the least bit funny.

And it *had* been a lot of work. But each day had brought a new adventure as he searched for another stone for the baby's garden. There were dragonflies to chase, goat dung to examine, abandoned birds' nests to collect. And each day it diverted him to Grandfather, so Nyere could rest in the oppressive afternoon heat.

"I hope the baby will like our garden," he sighed, in a tone that suggested it was unlikely that his work would be appreciated in equal measure to the effort he had afforded the task.

"How are *you* passing the time, Grandfather?" Chiumbo wondered, knowing it was an awfully long time to wait. Chilemba shook his head in amusement; how to explain that the wait seemed such a short time to him, when to a child it was interminable. So he did what elders in this position often do. He changed the subject.

"I have been preparing something for my other grandchild," he admitted. "You have done such hard work, preparing the stones. I have been working on a gift for you, to celebrate your eight rains."

"I suppose I must wait for this gift, as I must wait for the baby," Chiumbo grumbled, feeling acutely the idea that everything was being pushed aside for the baby.

"Unlike the baby, you are here now. Which is lucky because I am finished with it."

Chiumbo could scarce contain his excitement at this unexpected change of fortune, but never mind how carefully he looked, there was nothing in his grandfather's hands.

"Grandfather, you would not trick me, would you?" Chiumbo wondered.

"I might," Chilemba admitted, "but not this time."

And sure enough, when the boy looked again, he saw the spearhead in Grandfather's hands, and shrieked with pleasure.

"I think you are old enough to keep a secret, now," Grandfather's light brown eyes were searching the boy's face. "I do not think your mother believes that you are grown enough to think about what you have to defend, but if we wait for her, you will be a man, and I will be so old that I can no longer prepare such things."

Chiumbo heard none of this, simply threw his arms around Grandfather, feeling the rumble of the man's deep laughter where his face rested against Chilemba's chest, and thinking that this was nearly an adequate substitute to his mother's embrace.

3

CHIUMBO WAS AWAKENED FROM A happy slumber some nights later. He realized he was moving and opened his eyes. He discovered he was being carried in Father's arms.

"*Aba?*"

"Shhh." Gatimu's breath was warm against his ear. "The baby is coming, so you must come to sleep with me by the fire."

This statement brought the boy fully awake. How he had longed to spend the night away from the hut with the older boys and men. Perhaps Grandfather was right, and he was growing up, not the baby that his cousins still told him he was.

He could hear his mother's soft cries, and he grew worried, looking back toward the hut. "Is *Ama* going to be well?"

"All is well, my son," Father reassured him. "She must work with the other women to help the baby come into the world. She is speaking to the baby in its own language, to coax it out."

Father brought him to a place several paces outside of the village, finally setting him down near the signal fire. He indicated his bedroll, but Chiumbo was fully awake. He shook his head, not wanting to be disobedient. "*Please, Aba.*"

Gatimu said nothing, but his stern expression finally relented, understanding the excitement of the occasion. The other goatherders and some of the hunters were asleep around the fire, so Father indicated that any disturbances due to childish nonsense would not be tolerated.

Chiumbo spent this time happily exploring in the firelight, watching the wind move the long grasses, and shying away from the darkness that the firelight did not touch. This strange frenzy of adventurousness lasted only the better part of an hour, and by then the sky was lightening in the east, and he could no longer keep his eyes open.

He surrendered to strange dreams, and awakened to late morning sunshine when his slumbering mind realized that the hoofbeats of the zebras that ran through his imagination were really the running footsteps of one sent out from the beyond the huts. The fire had been banked for cooking, and Chiumbo looked around in sleepy confusion.

Although he did not hear what was said, the boy's face was distressed, and he turned back to the village as he spoke, with Gatimu on the run behind him. Father waved his arm to indicate that Chiumbo should stay behind.

But such excited activity could only herald the arrival of the baby, and Chiumbo stumbled to his feet and followed several paces behind.

When he arrived at the hut, he examined the faces of Grandfather and the *Shangazi*, not understanding why he read sorrow there and not joy. They tried to keep him from entering the hut, but he pushed past the forest of legs, calling for his *Ama*, wanting her to be all right, his voice dying in his throat when he skidded to a stop inside the doorway, seeing the strange expressions on the familiar faces of his parents.

Nyere gasped when she saw him, and put her hand over her mouth. "Chiumbo, you must not-" She made a gesture with her hand as if to push him back out of the hut and away.

"Bad luck, my son," Father shook his head sadly. "Go to your grandfather and pray. The *mganga* will come for her."

Chiumbo then caught a glimpse of the tiny bundle within Mother's arms. He was not entirely sure what his eyes were telling him, and before he got a good look, Nyere had turned away, shielding the baby from his view.

But Chiumbo had worked too hard, waited far too long to be discouraged from seeing his new sibling. He did not understand why *Ama* and *Aba* were so determined to keep him away, so he said, "The baby is mine, too, Father, isn't that what you promised?"

This time, his parents' eyes met, and although he did not understand what passed between them, he saw the fear in *Ama*'s expression, and she did not quite shake her head but implied her dissent in this. *Aba* sighed, but he nodded. "I did promise it, my son."

Chiumbo approached slowly, peering around his mother's shoulder, looking again at the baby. It was a girl, with curly hair, arms, legs, hands, feet. A face, pale as milk. *That* was unlike any other baby he had ever seen, but she was otherwise just like him. Was this what everyone was so upset about?

"May I hold her then? If she is also mine," he reasoned.

Nyere handed the baby to Gatimu, who looked down at her with shocked grief, his mouth twisted bitterly. Reluctantly, he settled the bundle in Chiumbo's arms. The baby wriggled, and pursed her lips in silent protest.

"Why is the *mganga* coming?" Chiumbo asked, not liking the feelings he was having. Suspicion, and fear. Mistrust, because no one was talking.

"Because the baby, our baby, was taken," Father explained. "This baby is a ghost, and she must be returned to the spirits. She is not really a person. The evil that left her could bring misfortune to all in our village."

Chiumbo heard something in his father's voice he had never heard before. He did not like it. He paid attention to the way it made him feel. It was something false, but without levity. There was no teasing in it. What he could not know is that he had heard the first of many lies he would hear in his life. Or perhaps not the first, but now that he was awake to deception, he would know its taste.

He was insulted that they did not think he was old enough for the truth, when he could so clearly recognize its opposite. He did not know which of the two things was worse.

He consulted his feelings. The baby had weight in his arms, and was hardly frightful. Her little mouth was as pretty as his own. He could feel her warmth against his belly, and when he bent close over her, her tiny hand reached out blindly and bumped against his face. It felt right, somehow.

There was a murmur outside the door that heralded the arrival of the *mganga*. The elders in the doorway parted to let him through, and he shuffled forward, his wizened face alight with greed, already looking for the baby. Reflexively, Chiumbo held her tighter.

The medicine man's expression reminded Chiumbo of an aged vulture, and he did not bother to hide the curved blade he carried as he leaned toward the newborn.

Chiumbo backed up slowly until he was pressed against the wall of the hut. He bent his face to the baby, and squinted, seeing her blurred features framed through his eyelashes and then tried to listen with his whole body, knowing there was not much time.

And when the *mganga* spoke, in that sweet, lulling, solicitous voice, crooning at the boy to give up the child, Chiumbo's heart showed him the truth. The eye magic had taught him that this baby was perfect, despite what his vision said, despite what everyone saw, despite her differences, his sister was…his sister. And while he knew not what it meant, he understood perfectly well what he must not do.

Holding her securely, he put his head down, and he ran.

4

CHIUMBO WENT BLINDLY, IGNORING THE ragged shouts of his neighbors as he escaped the crowd, unsure where to go.

His feet flew over the ground, and he knew he had to protect little sister, but suddenly he remembered what he had forgotten. It was a risk to turn back, but there was something he should not leave behind.

That errand done, he sprinted away through the long grass beyond the signal fire, passing the goats where they roamed, and into the unknown.

He did not stop running until his lungs were afire and he could not find another breath. He stooped over, leaning against the sandpapery trunk of an acacia, and held the baby against his chest. She was very pink from the heat, and had he understood in what peril she stood from the sun and the lack of hydration or milk, he might have despaired. His ignorance and blind faith served to drive him onward, not willing to relinquish hope, thinking of nothing but keeping her safe.

He knew he was small, that even his name meant "little one," and could sense his pursuers coming behind him, all bigger and stronger than he. He had other concerns, he was not old enough to know the land around him, his tiny village had, until now, been his whole world.

But he knew there were creatures about on the plains, and if they would steal a goat, surely they would make a meal of a boy and his sister. Luckily, those predators avoided the worst heat of the day, so he had some time. Until darkness fell, at least, to find shelter. Or so he believed.

He could not know that his human predators would be the biggest of his worries, and that their persistence was driven by a false belief, that the necessity of the infant's death precluded any argument to the contrary, that the fate of the village was predicated on her sacrifice.

But he felt the urgency in his bones. And began, again, to run.

He thought about his family. They had taught him how to use the magic, and in doing so, he feared they had lost their own. Perhaps this was all his fault. He had to do what he could save her.

He kept going, slowing steadily but imperceptibly, his exhaustion like a pack of hounds at his heels. And finally, when the long shadows stretched their hands toward him lovingly, they seemed to snag his clothing, holding him, inviting him to stop. Eventually, he did. He leaned into the shady enclosure among a stand of tall trees, and the whispering wind was like a lullaby. Chiumbo's head was too, too heavy, and when he could no longer hold it up, he slept, wedged there between the tree trunks, the baby sheltered by his cape.

His eyes opened only a few moments later, trying to make sense of what he saw. Across the clearing, Gatimu stood, and the familiarity of his face was almost a relief. His expression was both sad, and loving.

Chiumbo looked around, but although he could see none of the others, he knew they were there. He saw a storm out over the plains to the east, and the air was charged with the energy of an impending rainshower.

Gatimu approached, coming ever closer, and he held out his hands in front of himself, a gesture for calm. Chiumbo wanted nothing more than to fall into those arms, and be safe once more, but it was the false comfort of the childhood that he had shed somewhere on the plains that lay between him and home.

"That's close enough, *Aba*," he warned, although he knew, no, *believed* it to be an empty threat. If Father got close enough, Chiumbo was afraid he would give her up without a fight, a betrayal of not only his sister, but also himself.

"You must understand, my son," Father began, speaking in a soft voice as one would use with a child, but Chiumbo was no longer who he had been only that morning. It seemed so long ago.

"Understand lies, *Aba*? Understand murder?" Chiumbo said, and he gripped the baby more tightly in his right arm, flexing the fingers of his left hand around his other burden.

But before Gatimu could answer, there was another sound in the shadows behind the boy, a stealthy approach that Chiumbo was prepared for. He waited, holding his breath, pretending he had not heard it, and when the time was right, he swung his left hand back, the point of the spearhead aiming down and away, where it met the flesh of the *mganga's* thigh, opening up the muscle, before Chiumbo jerked it free, feeling and seeing the blood spatter against his side before he bounded away once more, praying for the flight of sister gazelle, calling on the wind for a push.

5

HE HAD ALLOWED THEM TO get too close, but the screams of the mganga slowed the men from the village for a few precious moments, and by the time the hunters returned to the chase, the thunder exploding overhead contributed to their confusion, abetting his escape.

Chiumbo crashed down a hill, using his free arm to shield his sister from the shrubs that slowed his descent. At the bottom, he saw he was in a gorge, mercifully shaded from the setting sun.

Lightning arced in the twilight sky and he glanced over his shoulders, crying out in a panic when he saw that his pursuers were only steps behind him. Tears sprung to his eyes as he realized his failure, and he followed the streambed that ran along the floor of the gorge, nearly stumbling in his desperation and panic. He kept his head down as he charged ahead, only looking up when his eye caught a flash of red color, the fabric of a cloak turning in the wind.

A woman stood directly in ahead of him, too close for him to avoid, and Chiumbo had no time to change course before he ran right into her, and felt a shock that almost made him drop the baby. But he held onto the child, and the woman held onto him, turning away, using his momentum to sweep him off his feet, and the world fell away.

***

Open your eyes, the voice whispered, but when Chiumbo complied, he felt sure that the command was only in his head.

Sunset was imminent, and dusk had advanced in the time he had lost. They were no longer in the stream bed, rather somewhere on the plains, and a full moon hung high to the east.

With a start, he remembered the baby, and gasped in relief when he looked down, confirming she was safe.

Again that fluttering red banner ahead, and he focused upon it, seeing it was a part of a larger form, a voluminous abaya the color of the clay of his home. It whipped over and around a luminous woman, who stood calmly in contemplation of the child looking back at her.

Up and up and up she went, impossibly tall, taller than all the men in the village, towering over him like a tree. Her platinum curls were a halo that matched those of the babe he carried, and seemed to be set against the sky. Her eyes were golden, like the cheetah's, infused with their own light. Her expression was one of polite interest. She said nothing. Nothing at all. Her beauty he could see clearly, and she had a goodness he could feel.

The hair on his arms stood up, the air charged still with the storm, he thought, but the sky had cleared. Then he remembered the energy that had flowed from her when they collided. It gave him hope.

He stopped for a moment to listen, indeed he turned around in a complete circle, taking in the horizon, the empty plain, the curvature of the earth, the darkening bowl of the sky. His pursuers were gone.

"Do you know about magic?" Chiumbo swallowed hard against his fear and asked the question, and although she did not reply, her expression changed slightly. He thought he saw curiosity there, and amusement.

He stammered on, "Goddess, I used the eye magic on her. She is perfect. I cannot take care of her. Can you save her?" He held the baby out, with a certainty that comforted him, a confidence he had not felt before that moment.

When she did not immediately reach for the bundle, he showed her the contents of his left hand, uncurling his fingers. He had clutched it so tightly that it had sliced open both sides of his palm.

Kusini looked at the blood he had sacrificed, some his own, and some another's. She took the spearhead that he presented her, and he sighed in relief, knowing his offering was acceptable.

"What is her name?" Again, Chiumbo, in his exhaustion, could not discern whether that papery whisper came from this messenger of the heavens, or from his mind.

"What day is it?" he asked. "Is it still the first day?"

Kusini nodded, smiling down at him, then raised an eyebrow, expectantly anticipating his answer.

"She is Jumapi'li," he replied, and the baby seemed to smile.

Chiumbo barely felt her touch as she lifted the infant from his arms. Then she touched him on the shoulder, and the plains receded as the sun slipped away.

He opened his eyes under the milky band of the stars, hearing the sounds of the village beyond the grass where he lay, alone once more.

6

Memory seemed to have left them alone, those unfortunate members of his village; perhaps it was a mercy he was not meant to share. Only Chiumbo remembered it all, and in spite of his deliverance, he did not regret that his own knowledge of those events remained intact.

And he kept the magic that allowed him to see, truly see those around him, but now the Great Secret only made him sad, it did not hold the promise that it once had. Seeing others for who they really are is both a great responsibility and an even greater burden. You must carry silently your disappointment in those you love. In his case, they did not even recall the grievous injury they had done him.

Chiumbo grew into the man he was meant to be, a husband, a father, a goatherder, a villager. But though he was led in his decisions by his heart, and was heralded for his kindness, and knew much joy, and was loved, he was not complete, and he feared he never would be.

He tarried longer and longer on the evening plains, contemplating the sun as it sank from view, looking out to the east, to that place, in another world, in another life. Still he wondered, always he wondered.

And on a summer evening, much like that one before, there was something new, emerging from the western plain, but his vision failed him, inadequate in the brightness.

He remembered the eye magic, squinting until he saw only his lashes, and then, a shadow coalesced, outlined against the shimmering orb of the setting sun. It revealed a person, and Chiumbo saw that it made the same silhouette that any other human would.

He watched until his eyes ached, and the light spots in his vision danced, but it was no hallucination. Advancing toward him over the plain was a woman, and at first it seemed that his angel had returned, but he breathed into the silence, and his heart said no, this was a being of the earth, no celestial inhabitant of a fevered dream.

Her sandals kicked up the red dust as she approached, her gait that of Nyere, but their mother she was not. The burden in her arms was unmistakable, and she did not stop walking until she was close enough to touch him.

"Brother," she greeted him warmly, her eyes of liquid gold had flecks of green, he saw. And they were lit with amusement, gratitude, happiness. On a leather thong about her slim, proud neck, she wore his spearhead.

She turned aside to show him what she carried, her son, his skin the ebon hue of his uncle, rather than the pale radiance of his mother. He looked down upon this miracle, made possible out of his refusal to turn away from truth. The circle of life, unbroken by the destructions of suspicion and fear. And suddenly, Chiumbo wept, tears of joy, tears of understanding, finally able to make sense of it all.

She placed a gentle hand on his shoulder, and pulling her necklace from her throat, returned the talisman to its rightful owner. Chiumbo looked at her questioningly.

Off in the distance, he thought he glimpsed a swirling banner of red cloth, the raiment of the Goddess, and Jumapi'li said, "Your debt to the gods is paid as you have continued to believe in the magic, and to teach it to others who need to know it."

encumbrance

kilbuck mountain wilderness
north of tuluksak, alaska territory
1945

1918, Lower Kalskag

Aata taught him to kill.

It seemed that killing was the only thing that interested Cold Bear's father, the only way that he made sense of the world.

Cold Bear wanted to make sense of the world, too, but he could not understand what Aata expected of him, knew he was a disappointment. He followed his father through the woods, watching the proud straight back striding on and on through the forest.

He often wondered what would happen if he stopped walking altogether, and just sat down, in the snow, right there in the middle of the trail. Father never looked back, and Cold Bear knew better than to speak unless it was demanded of him, so he guessed that his absence could go unnoticed for a long time.

But he knew that there would be consequences; Father expected him to be there, where he always was, ready to listen. Not that he had a choice, Aata never really talked to anyone, he talked at them. Cold Bear still had a child's blind faith that someone would look for him.

But then he remembered that Aana was gone, so perhaps no one would. While this thought was sobering, for Cold Bear the possibility that his father would find him gone and not bother to look for him gave him a small feeling of fatalistic joy. Perhaps yet he had the power to do something. He could disappear, and if Winter claimed him, maybe he would be free of his failures.

But he had to own the knowledge that there was another possibility, one that involved beatings. And another diatribe about how Cold Bear was even stupider than Aata had imagined him to be.

So he trudged onward, secretly hoping that they would not encounter any game. Sadly certain that they would.

Father was not frustrated in his efforts, and after a few hours more, there was furtive movement up ahead in the trees. Aata signaled to Cold Bear to stay behind, out of sight, and watch. Cold Bear immediately dropped to a crouch and held his position, not wanting to give Father any reason to blame him if the quarry were lost.

His father's prey turned out to be a skinny lone wolf, on its own fruitless hunting expedition. Father always said killing another predator was more of a challenge, because they had greater intelligence, and this poor animal was also desperate due to hunger and want. The vicious sounds it made may have been due to the ravages of some illness, but as Cold Bear listened and remained out of sight, its cries became a song of agony, as the animal was teased and tortured before his father ended its misery.

Senseless. It was not really an animal that they could eat. Its coat could be used for many things, but Cold Bear knew they would not be taking that away with them either. He knew Father had a sickness, but there was no one he could tell of this. And if he could, there was no cure for it.

When it was over, he moved from his hiding place and joined Aata. Father always wanted him to witness his victories, and participate in the collection of trophies and the ritual that invariably followed.

The wolf lay ripped open on the snow, its blue eyes staring in what Cold Bear felt was a raw accusation, its muzzle spattered with its own blood. Father had gutted it, and was pulling the heart from its attachments. He ate some of it, and offered the rest to Cold Bear, who knew better than to refuse.

Aata handed him a heavy stone, and nodded toward the poor creature. Cold Bear took the stone, not seeing any alternative, and bashed in the animal's skull while his father waited impatiently. All the while, the beast's eyes still seemed to watch him.

"If you can best an animal that has intelligence, cunning, and strength, you gain its qualities. You show your worth by establishing yourself in superiority over it," his father intoned, beginning a familiar speech. "It is no challenge to trap or hunt a lesser animal. When you achieve victory over a worthy opponent, you prove yourself a god. When you ingest its mind, you gain its powers."

Cold Bear tried to tune out the words he had heard so many times before, finally breaching the cranium. He pushed his fingers into the soft brain, knowing that Father's careful eye was on him, his expectations clear. Cold Bear scooped the tissue into his mouth and tried to control his revulsion at his participation in something he knew was a crime against nature, performing this false duty that Aata deemed necessary. All the while thinking that perhaps the fate of the animal was better than his own.

They never said the prayers of thankfulness for the animal's sacrifice, not this one or any other. Cold Bear worried that they could anger the spirits of this forest, that Raven's eye would find them, judge them, and damn them.

On the way home, they met a man crossing the ice at the narrowest part of the river. He carried a string of burbot over his shoulder; he had likely come from downstream near the tributaries, and looked to be returning from ice fishing.

He was tall, even taller than Father, wearing mukluqs of seal fur that had unfamiliar tribal markings and a parka made from a bearskin. His hood was down, his long hair pooling in it, save for a single tiny braid that snaked over his left shoulder and rested on his chest.   As they passed him, Aata did not bother to stand aside, bumping him significantly with a hard shoulder. The man turned, and paused, looking thoughtfully at Father and then at Cold Bear with strange eyes that were too much like the eyes of the wolf they had slain, cold and blue, with large, dark, depthless centers. Cold Bear wondered if the spirits had caught up with them, if they knew of the murders of their animal brethren.

The man said nothing, but sniffed the air and frowned, giving Father a significant look, a dangerous look, baring his teeth for a moment, involuntarily, revealing the unnaturally sharp lateral incisors at the angles of his mouth. It was subtle, but Cold Bear felt something, knew that perhaps this man was not really a man.

And Cold Bear saw something else. Aata was suddenly afraid. And knew that his son recognized it, was witness to this insult. So he looked down at the ground and tried to pretend he did not understand the significance of the challenge that had passed from this man to his father. Pretend he did not notice that for all his talk, Father backed down immediately. Instinctively Cold Bear knew that whatever price was to be paid for his father's humiliation, he would be the one to pay it.

Cold Bear also did not see the relief in the other man's eyes that he would not have to expend any violence in front of the boy. For Amaoke had recognized the anguish in the child's dark eyes, and could separate the sharp smell of his fear, and the lingering scent of longstanding terror that permeated the skins he wore, from the stink of the butchered wolf that clung to his father. He saw that the boy's path was already fraught with suffering, and he refused to add to his pain.

So he gave the other man his back in response, striding away into the woods to see what he could do to restore some dignity to his fallen brother.

1

1945

THE CHILL ATE THROUGH THE thin jean jacket he wore, but he tried to ignore it. He needed a better coat, and probably a hat, but like so many others this first autumn following the end of the war, Amaoke's needs outstripped his means. Even if he did not need to hold on to what little money he had, supply did not meet demand in the larger cities, let alone middle America.

He had been fortunate enough to find four day's work picking fruit at the harvest. A few of the other men in the crew were Apsáalooke, and they must have recognized the challenges he faced at every turn, finding work, securing lodging. Although he was still an oddity, outcast in society as neither one thing or another, they recognized that he shared their struggle, and one of them invited him home. He was grateful, but other than agreeing to accept the hospitality of having a roof over his head, he refused to take their food, seeing the big eyes and empty bellies of the man's children. Indeed, he left them the bruised, half-rotten apples he had been allowed to collect off the ground at the farm in grateful payment. Perishables were dear, but there was still plenty of wildlife, and he had never gone hungry.

The dry goods store in Bozeman had very little clothing to choose from, certainly nothing in his size. The proprietor's wife had been kind to him, and he could smell her sadness. It seemed to be everywhere, this grief, not yet tinged by hopefulness brought by the end of world conflict, and there was yet to be any indication of economic recovery.

She had offered him the jacket with a small shake of her head. "It's the biggest we have." When he put the money for it on the counter, she looked at it and pushed some of it back toward him. "That jacket is on sale."

He left the money where it lay. "I'm obliged to you, ma'am, but please keep it. Maybe someone is coming after me who needs it more than I do. You see that they get it."

He was getting a later start than he wanted, had meant to get North before the cold, but travel was slow and difficult. It was hard to find anyone willing to pick him up, so he had done a fair bit of walking. Stowing on trains was getting harder and harder. He knew he might need to abandon the jacket for his winter fur sooner rather than later, so it would do. It made him sad to think there were humans who would brave the Montana winter without much else.

A trucker in Boulder gave him a ride to Great Falls. Two days later, a logging outfit headed into Alberta agreed to let him ride in their empty truck. He wrapped his hair around his neck and over his ears, and pressed himself up against the back of the cab to take the best advantage of the windbreak.

There was snow when they reached Milk River, and he parted ways with his transport. It took the better part of the next ten days to reach Whitehorse. The cold was insidious; the day he arrived one could have believed that there was still time to prepare for winter, but when the sun went away and Wind came down out of the Dawsons, there could be no mistake. In those northern climes, October looks nothing like its idyllic counterpart in the lower territories. He had waited too long, and he knew he would suffer for it.

He left the jacket and his boots in the outdoor restroom of a petrol station north of Haines Junction, hoping someone who could use them would find them, and then the full moon was upon him, and humanity was lost. So Amaoke left the man behind and headed for home on four legs.

2

IT WAS PAST HIS BIRTHDAY when he reached the river to the north of Tuluksak, a skinny, exhausted wolf. Much of his diet had consisted of small rodents and the occasional unlucky bird.

He had seen other wolves, traveling south in packs, and considered joining them. He was amused by the irony; they were wise enough to follow their food; his human side complicated the Wolf's pragmatism. He wanted to be home. Home would mean hungry this terrible winter, when no one had enough.

But he gave the alphas a wide berth, and when that was not enough, and their curious calls came down through the trees, he answered them, warned them away with the hungry scream of the berserker. They were smart enough to put distance between their families and him after that, for which he was glad. He had, in his advanced years, lost his appetite for dominance battles, recognizing them as wasteful where he was concerned. He was strong enough to lead and protect, but had no capacity to procreate, and thus his displays of power robbed his brethren of the gift of new life, continued bloodlines. It went against Nature's rules. So he avoided it when he was able, and no longer took his comfort hiding among them as a rule.

Off the river, there was a hunting camp, surprisingly occupied, probably by a prospector. There were sled dogs sheltered among the trees, and someone had left a fishy *akutaq* for them. He darted in and guiltily stole some of it before melting back into the woods, their indignant howls bringing their humans. It was unfair of him to take their food, and he felt for them, constantly tied up, unable to run free. But they traded their freedom for shelter and regular meals, which was a tempting compromise even for Amaoke at that moment.

Another half day's travel upriver brought him to its narrow point in the shadow of the Kilbuck mountains, so he crossed on the ice and headed away from the water, into the near foothills. Although the land had changed subtly, as it did so close to the ever-changing path of the river, he found the familiar clearing ringed by gargantuan pines, and bounded happily through the snow, knowing that he was finally home.

It seemed that every time he left, he told himself he would not stay away long, but then sometimes as much as a century would pass before he realized how much he missed this part of the world. It struck him that its pull was likely a combination of many things, the strongest of which was that it was the place where he had once been loved, innocent of the burden of his forced duality.

Beyond the trees, the land rose slightly, transforming into a forest bluff that he traversed until his nose was able to reorient itself to the landscape. It took him only the better part of an hour to pick up the scent that he was searching for.

The cave had changed little over the intervening centuries and he found it much as he had left it, albeit used by transient animal inhabitants over the years. He approached it with caution, and was pleased to find it empty, but did stop to wonder why the bears had passed up the opportunity to spend the winter's hibernation in such a shelter.

Once he had located it again, he backtracked along a familiar circuit, leaving a scent message to the other animals before formally marking the cave as his own.

Bracing himself, he used the curve beyond the opening as protection from the elements and forced the Wolf to accept the change back to man. It was an emotional and physical struggle that his animal brother almost won.

He shivered in the freezing air, but to take advantage of the cave's best feature required opposable thumbs. When he reached along the high, natural shelf in the rock wall opposite the opening, his hand first felt the walrus-skin pouch that held his mother's *ulu*. He was glad that whatever magic governed his life returned it here to be rediscovered on the many occasions in which he had lost it, or simply had to leave it behind.

The magic also variably supplied him with other blessings, so he stood on tiptoe and reached as far as he could, his fingers plunging into the softness of a pelt. He scissored his long fingers to pinch a bit of it, but it was too heavy to capture that way. He tried to add a bit of a jump, and on the third try, he finally succeeded in snagging the large bundle, only paying for it with a half yard of the skin under his arm.

The sacrifice was worth it, as the bundle contained *mukluqs* that looked suspiciously similar to the ones that Iniẍ had fashioned for him long ago, and a warm bear parka and pants that could have been the duplicates of ones he had worn in these woods a few decades prior. There were also some marmot and woodchuck skins, and some dried fish, an unusual bounty. Perhaps the spirits knew in what terrible shape he would have been without clothing, and at least something of worth to trade.

3

HE DELAYED THE TRIP BACK into Tuluksak for three days while he set up a new hunting camp in the shadow of the pines to the north of the clearing, prepared his fire pit, and did a bit of general exploring.

When he was satisfied with these initial arrangements, he retraced his journey south, planning to find a place in town to trade furs for seal oil, and perhaps other essentials. He was grateful for a dry journey with no snow, but he knew that meant his return was likely to be difficult. The harsh weather never held off for long at these latitudes.

The general store also served as a post office and rendezvous point for gold prospectors and missionaries who were headed north. When Amaoke arrived, he was not entirely surprised to see that the town had grown significantly in the past thirty years.

He pulled the front door, triggering the clang of the bell hanging above it, but before he could step inside, he was muscled out of the way by a mountain of a man on his way out. Amaoke paused in surprise, as much from the man's scent as the physical rudeness, which he knew some weaker men used to assert a false dominance.

The man was easily half a hand taller than Amaoke, and likely outweighed him by a significant factor. Amaoke recognized his scent, meaning that he'd met this person in a previous encounter, but he was unable to immediately place him. He was the type of person one did not easily forget. And he smelled something else on his person, something infinitely more ominous, and if his nose served him, frankly disturbing.

Amaoke stared after him thoughtfully, but his assailant did not turn back or acknowledge the event in any observable way.

"Ignore Angus. It's the wisest course." The proprietor had witnessed the exchange, and Amaoke privately agreed with him. It wasn't worth the effort.

"Angus?" Amaoke repeated the name, tasted it. The man had clearly been of the First People, and this name was unexpected.

"Ayuh. Angus Cold Bear," the man explained, his accent that of a New Englander, although his countenance marked him as an Aleut, perhaps an Athabascan. "Angus is his *Christian* name. The missionaries took him off to school, but it was probably too late for him, you know. His father was legendarily crazy, and Angus was orphaned, but those religious folk didn't know how to care for him. At that point I don't imagine anyone could. They kept him long enough to saddle him with that name and sent him back when they couldn't control him."

Amaoke thought he heard some pity in that tone, so he listened as the man continued, "He lives some ways out in the Kilbuck Wilderness, which is probably a blessing. He's a bit of a bully, but probably more bark than bite."

Although Amaoke knew from what the brief encounter had told him that this man was sorely mistaken, he kept his peace. He suspected he was hearing so much of another's business on purpose, a not-so-subtle but polite warning. It would be otherwise unneighborly to reveal so much to a stranger.

"I'm Oscar Tachiqala," he said, revealing that he was one of the renamed as well. Amaoke found it difficult to get used to, and he knew that the name changes came with forced rehoming and placement of indigenous children in church schools, where they were forbidden to use their own languages, and in some cases to see their families again, in the name of a Christian charity that they could have done without. He knew some of them disappeared altogether, and the missions were short on explanations as to why.

"Amaoke," he introduced himself, with a genuine smile.

"You're new around here," Oscar observed unnecessarily. "In town to do some trading?"

Amaoke nodded.

"That's a beautiful coat." Oscar admired it for a few moments, then added, "There are plenty around here who would be interested in a skin like that."

"Bear Woman would hunt me down if I tried to barter with it," Amaoke laughed. "I've got some nice marmot and muskrat skins, though."

These he placed on the counter as Oscar nodded. "My wife is like that, too," he commiserated, and Amaoke was amused at his assumption but did not bother to correct him. He thought of Nanatha. What he wouldn't give for her scolding now. As his mind started to wander off task, he realized that Oscar was talking again and gave the man his attention once more.

"These are really nice. You need seal oil?"

"And a few other things," Amaoke gestured to the dry goods.

"Yeah. Feel free to find what you need. We'll settle up at the end," Oscar told him with a smile.

When Amaoke was concluding his transaction, Oscar commented, "Your eyes are so striking, and I realized why I noticed them. They look familiar. There was another fur trader in these parts awhile back, got to be thirty years or more. I think it was the first summer I got back from…" His eyes misted over, reminiscing, and then he shook his head as if shaking off a bad memory. "Anyway, I was helping out in here. My pa ran the place back then. Fella had eyes just like yours."

"My father was trapping here in the teens, I think," Amaoke lied. "Up in Kalskag or thereabouts."

"Must have been," Oscar nodded, then shook his head in amazement. "You sure favor him."

"That I do." Amaoke could not help but smile, and then he sketched a wave and took his leave.

4

AMAOKE SPENT MILDER DAYS TREKKING along the river to drop, maintain, and harvest from his ice fishing lines. On days when the wind and snow howled and swirled around the camp, he cured meat from his traps and sewed hides. Some days were neither one nor the other, and in those odd limbos, he searched the forest floor for an old cache of whalebone struts that he had saved from half a century before. He found them under the snow, behind a line of trees where the reclining maiden had once been the singular feature of his meadow home. He spent several days clearing the snow and excavating the ones that had started to sink into the soil. Most of them had been kept reasonably near the surface atop the ubiquitous pine needles that blanketed the ground.

He planned to rebuild a dwelling and settle for a time. Subsistence living suited him, and his duality was best served within this forest, where he suspected his particular magic was concentrated, where the spirits generally supported his efforts, even in lean years.

It was never easy, but it kept him occupied, body and soul. Mind, too. It had been less than a human lifetime since he had lost Nanatha. He found that without her, he had no particular desire to be part of society. He knew he was hiding from his life, knew she would disapprove, but here in this wilderness he could pretend to forget about a life he'd had that now felt like a distant dream.

A dream that stayed at the edges of his consciousness, invaded his slumber, but was lost with no small amount of pain on waking. He still reached for her beside him. His arms ached for the emptiness they found.

So if life on the river was harsh, so be it. He would blunt one deprivation with a multitude of others.

One evening, returning with his fish catch, he had just turned upriver and crossed from the west to the east bank on the icy bridge that marked the path home when the forest's peace was shattered with a piercing scream of agony.

Amaoke was still, listening again for more, shocked because it sounded human, although he knew that there were other creatures whose calls could mimic a person. They had been the stuff of nightmares when he was a boy.

He could hear shouts of pain from deeper in the woods, and he dropped his burdens and started to run toward them. As he got closer the sounds had subsided to the gasps and whistles of one who is going into shock, and as he had not scented or seen any other people in his woods, he was wary.

There was a clearing up ahead, and in the dusky gloom that marked the dark of the year, he could see movement, the struggles of some sort of large animal caught in a trap. He inched forward cautiously, looking around carefully at his own feet before stopping.

He put his nose to work, and it did not make him happy. It was a man caught in a steel jaw trap, which seemed to have been set right on one of the natural trails that trappers used to enter the wilderness east of the water. It was less than a seven-minute walk from his own camp. He could smell the oiled metal, and old blood, but not animal blood, this was the putrefaction of several layers of human blood, from more than one unfortunate person. And it was different from the blood of the individual currently in the trap.

Amaoke could see the man's anguish, and he worried. He sat still, and breathed in deeply. The man smelled of pine, and of his diet of root vegetables, berries, and small rodents. A trapper certainly, not indigenous, and older, a whitebeard with papery wrinkled skin. His breath came in and out in gasps and tears ran down his face.

His right leg was caught in the trap, broken, the skin and deeper flesh mangled and bleeding. He would die if Amaoke did not help him. He smelled nothing untrustworthy about the man, so he stepped out of the woods.

He understood it when the older gentleman flinched away from him; he was aware of the fierceness of his visage. Up here, in this untamed place, you counted other people enemy long before you decided they were friend.

"I heard your screams," he explained, in as gentle a tone as he could, kneeling in the snow next to the trail.

"I-I-I didn't know this was your land," the man was hyperventilating, and his words came out in hiccupping gasps. "I'm s-sorry I set off your trap."

Amaoke thought it was extraordinary that this man would be worried about apologizing when his life was in danger. He ignored it, saying only, "The land belongs to no man. You are welcome to pass here. This is not my trap."

And examining the contraption, he frowned. It was a heavy thing, even meaner than the one he had found himself caught in long ago. A bear trap. With the scents of human injury and human death? Everything about it was wrong. He felt for the trapper; another day and Amaoke himself could have been the victim.

He released the spring and freed the man's leg, but this just brought more wound exposure and bleeding. Using sheer strength, enough to startle the trapper at least, he tore a length from his buckskin sleeve and wrapped the leg as tightly as possible.

"You have a camp near here?" Amaoke asked. "Mine is close, but if yours is closer to town, we should try to get there. You'll need to get into Tuluksak as soon as possible, but it wouldn't be wise to attempt it tonight, you wouldn't survive it."

"My homestead's just north of there," the man nodded. "About a forty-minute walk south once you cross the river there at the bend. But if you don't mind my sayin' so, I don't see how you're fixin' to get me there."

"Leave that to me," Amaoke said, and with a grunt that was more for the other man's benefit than from the pain of any real exertion, he hefted him aloft, putting him across his shoulders and pressing upward to get to his feet. He did not want to leave the trap behind, but the spring was pulled and set to, so at least it could not create any more casualties for now.

He liked to collect such weapons and keep them out of the hands of those who would dare use them here. And in this case, he felt it was especially prudent to do so. He turned back toward the river, and picked up the faintest unpleasantness on the wind. What he smelled did not surprise him, rather confirmed something he had already suspected. They were watched.

"What shall I call you, friend?" the man asked, obviously uncomfortable. "I'm Case Ellis, came up here to the territory from downstate after my wife died." His words came out in a jumble of delirium, almost the beginning of a rant.

Kindred spirits, thought Amaoke. "You can call me Amaoke," he said, then added, "You might want to save your breath. This isn't going to be a pleasant walk, but I will do my best to get you settled for the night, and then into town at first light."

5

Turned out, Ellis' homestead was the one with the sled dogs. Though they recognized Amaoke's scent, and barked in protest when he emerged from the woods, they settled down when they scented their owner. He knew they understood that something was wrong; they, like he, could smell the anguish, pain, and blood on their master, so they quieted quickly.

He wasted no time getting a fire started, and set the old man down near it to warm him up quickly while he gathered snow from outside to heat water for his wounds.

When he inquired about antiseptic, Ellis pointed him in the direction of the shelves near the cookstove, where he found some kind of firewater. Ellis smiled sheepishly and shrugged. When Amaoke moved to pour the liquid on the wounds, Ellis stayed his hands a moment and gently took the bottle from him.

"Just need a pull for courage," he moaned, trying to make a joke, and failing. Amaoke did not blame him. He hoped his intervention had been early enough and effective enough to help. Ellis looked twenty years older after their walk through the woods, and his face was pale and sweaty.

Amaoke used just enough to clean the wound and then wrapped the old trapper's shaking hands around the bottle. He took off his own heavy coat and wrapped the man in it, ignoring his protests.

He asked about food, and would not hear Ellis' refusals, finding squirrel stew in a pot behind the icehouse door, which he heated. He made the man take several bites of the rich broth, and Amaoke had to admit it was rather tasty. Later, he made peace with the dogs by giving them the remainder of the stew before he banked the stove coals and closed up the hut for the night.

The next morning they set out into a bitterly cold but blessedly clear day, and made good time to town. The leg did not look good, and both the doc and (more privately) Amaoke were predicting a need for its removal. Amaoke was saddened. He did not want Ellis to die, and if the leg festered either ahead of or after an amputation, it would not bode well for one so apparently fragile.

He made his promises to care for the dogs, and relocated to the hut in the woods for a time to see what fate would bring. He burned the *ayuq* and the *tarvaq* that showed up in the cave one day, thinking it was a provident reminder to remember old prayers. He sincerely asked the spirits to bring good medicine to his new friend.

Ellis did his part, and was stubbornly tough, and despite his fatalistic sighs about being too old to be 'worth a tick on a hound's backside,' he mended, and kept the leg, but it would prevent him from trapping on foot ever again. He reckoned he could use the dogs to create a circuit off the western side of the river, and continue to care for himself. Amaoke admired this independent spirit very much.

Amaoke liked him, and had to admit that he had become rather fond of the dogs, who remained understandably wary of him, but were relations of a sort. He had resisted the urge to set them all free, and he admitted this jokingly to Ellis, thankful especially because the dogs would have to be his legs from now on. But Ellis laughed, too, and had said he'd thought of it a time or two before his accident.

"They say those woods are haunted," he told Amaoke one night after they had shared a dinner of fresh fish pulled from the icy river just that day. The hut was cozy, the small space warmed by the cookstove's heat. There was an odd look in his eyes, a directness there that Amaoke found meaningful.

"And do you believe it?" Amaoke asked carefully. He had a balanced experience with spirits in this forest, but white men were not usually so in tune with the land, had their own form of spirituality. And he knew the stories. Some of them were old legends, from a time that was less civilized, and some of the stories were true. Like the one about a berserker who ruled this wilderness for a hundred years. Others were just ghost stories and tall tales.

"Not in haints and such," Ellis said. "But a lot of people have gone missing in these parts. Not all of 'em tenderfoots. Plenty of natives, including women and children – and they aren't out trapping, they don't come to the hunting camps. They are out in the daylight, working the fish camps, picking berries. They know the land better than any of the come-latelies." He stared into the fire.

"It's been ten years since my wife died," he finally said, leaning on his cane and tossing another log into the breech. Then he seemed to let himself follow that tangent. "You ever married?"

Amaoke did not trust himself to speak right away, so he nodded. Ellis passed him some dried fish, seeing Amaoke's expression, perhaps sensing that there was some pain there. Amaoke said, "I lost her some years ago."

"Hurts, don't it?" Ellis asked, the sadness in his voice so pervasive and so deep that Amaoke felt they were of the same heart about it.

"Like losing an arm, and never recovering," Amaoke replied honestly, and Ellis nodded. But he gave Amaoke a wise look and then spoke again.

"So, goin' on ten years I been rattlin' around these woods. When I first settled, you'd see wolves come down through the hollows, out along the foothills, and I had to watch the dogs, you know? Had to be careful gathering berries and honey certain times of year, because there were bears in that wilderness, too.

"Last five, six years now, don't see many predators. And it's not as if the prey animals have come back in force because of it. These woods are too quiet by half. I think it's because there is an extremely dangerous kind of predator out there. One that got tired of hunting four-legged killers and maybe's going after the two-legged kind."

Amaoke said nothing.   He did not tell Ellis that when he had scented Angus Cold Bear in town, he had identified him as a flesh-eater. The man stank of old terror and his scent could not hide his diet of humans. Nor did he share with Ellis that he had started tracking this evil, trying to locate its hiding place, following the clues it left behind.

Instead, he said, "I've found an average of three traps a month since you got caught. All the same kind. Built to catch a bear. Outlawed this far south. But modified for another purpose."

"I'm ashamed to say I suspected it," Ellis said. "But I'm too old to be taking on such a thing at my age. Or so I tell myself so's I don't have to admit I am a coward. Got to admit when I saw you comin' out of the trees I thought it was over. Turns out you're harmless," he teased, and then continued, "The authorities don't seem to be interested in interfering. But there are a number of folk who come out here to disappear, and they aren't so easy to be found."

"They are afraid, the lawmen and the elders alike," Amaoke correctly observed. "And they don't have enough information to go on." But he did. The traps he had scented were all marked with evidence of multiple kills. The hunter could only be setting traps for humans with them, because that was the only prey that could not smell all that death and instinctively avoid capture.

He had watched some of the traps for hours on end, watched prey animals giving them a wide berth, smelling the death and decay that painted the metal. And Amaoke had found the traps just using his nose. No self-respecting creature would go near the stink of fear and dead humans. He said none of this to Ellis.

It meant that Cold Bear was *only* trying to catch and kill one species. He had graduated from the sport of it, Amaoke surmised, or had deteriorated enough mentally, that he had decided to eat them, too.

6

HE FOUND FOUR MORE TRAPS during his ongoing searches, confident that he was on the right track. Late one grey, cold afternoon, when he was disabling the latest one he had found and was readying it for removal, the wind changed direction, and he realized he was no longer alone in that part of the forest.

Amaoke had the advantage of being able to smell his pursuer before he could see him, so he turned to the woods behind himself and said, "I know you are there."

The sounds of breaking branches heralded the man's path out of the woods. He did not bother to follow the trail around, simply came through the trees, forcing his way onward. Amaoke recognized it as an intimidation tactic, and refused to react. He simply stood his ground and waited for the confrontation.

"You cannot steal from my traps without consequences," Cold Bear snarled angrily, not stopping until he was close enough for Amaoke to feel the man's foul breath on his face.

"I took nothing from this trap. It was empty when I found it," Amaoke's calm, reasonable tone, and his refusal to be intimidated was infuriating to the other man, he could see, so he kept on. "Those traps of yours are illegal in this wilderness, illegal south of the Yukon territory. The tribal authorities might find their use interesting as well."

"Well, you *did* take a man out of one of those traps. I was following you," Cold Bear countered.

"I decided I wasn't going to let you eat him," the register of Amaoke's voice dropped slightly, and Cold Bear heard the challenge, and seemed somewhat astonished that Amaoke knew this. "I've been tracking *you*, too."

"This isn't your forest, and you took what was mine. But no matter. You can take his place." Cold Bear's fist shot out with a quickness that Amaoke was not prepared for, viciously connecting with Amaoke's face. The force behind that blow was tremendous, and the world went black.

When Amaoke regained consciousness, he was disoriented, and groggy. It took him a moment to remember where he was supposed to be. The forest was sliding by at an odd angle, and he realized that he was being dragged along an old caribou path by a stout rope that was tied around his ankles. His hands were also secured by another length of rope, and he slid along on his back, pulled behind a nightmare.

He shook his head to try and clear it, but if Cold Bear noticed he was awake he gave no indication of it. The man's punch had been so effective in short circuiting his consciousness that Amaoke's instinct to call the wolf had not even been triggered. He shuddered. He had been defenseless for the time he had been unconscious. He hurt everywhere, but was not yet certain the extent of his pain was explained by his current predicament.

When he looked more closely at his captor, what he saw worried him. Cold Bear had transformed, trading his winter clothing for the skin of a large Kodiak bear. The animal's head balanced atop Cold

Bear's own, and he had bathed in human blood. Amaoke could smell it, and he could see the red streaks on his legs and torso as he walked. It was still wet, dripping onto the snow. He wore foot coverings made from the feet of the animal, the claws dragging thin furrows on the trail.

He smelled something else, the scent of his own entrails. His enemy had pierced his gut with something, the blood he wore Amaoke's, like a sacrifice.

And Cold Bear was talking, whether to himself or to Amaoke it was impossible to tell, just a stream of conscious thought, the insane raving of the mad, "…taken from me, my food, so you will be my food…and I will swallow your death and your power, for I know you…" It sounded frighteningly like a prayer.

Amaoke recognized that the spirits could be returning this punishment for Bear Woman's death. Perhaps the Morningstar would let this psychopath take Amaoke's gifts into himself, and this sacrifice, this witchcraft, would give the Morningstar a more malleable and more devastating killer. He shivered. Cold Bear's madness would leave no barrier for resistance. The man could walk in his skin to do the Monster's bidding. He was surprised that the imbalance had not summoned the *Ungalek*, for this was a madness that could call the Death Bringer to the natural world.

Relentlessly, on and on they went, climbing into the mountains now, and despite the increasing grade, Cold Bear's steps were resolute, his pull on the rope inexorable.

Amaoke drifted in and out of consciousness, and in moments of clarity he wondered whether his death on this trail would be more peaceful than whatever Cold Bear ultimately had planned for him. He tried to focus on the pain, make it work for him, keep himself awake, try to keep his head aloft enough to avoid smashing against the boulders and trees along the path.

And then he saw her, disappearing and reappearing between the trees. A beautiful grey wolf, sometimes here, sometimes there. He could not say she was not a vision brought on by cold and blood loss. Cold Bear did not seem to notice her. Interestingly, Amaoke could not scent her.

Yet the message was delivered. Amaoke felt hope; he might not die on this day.

Brother Iraluk was low in the sky but would not be leaving them, a sliver of brightness that was not enough to call the wolf. They had arrived at a clearing about halfway up the face of the mountain when Cold Bear finally dropped the rope and Amaoke came to rest.

Cold Bear turned to him, and Amaoke wondered what the other people he had killed had seen before they died. A madman wearing Bear's clothing, assuming Bear's devastating, destructive power. Had they known he was going to eat them? Amaoke was sure they had.

"I know what you are," the man's fevered eyes looked for any sign of fear in his victim, but Amaoke refused him the satisfaction.

"You'll take no pleasure from my death," Amaoke told him, steeling himself to control his fear, dampen any emotional reactions. He needed to keep a clear head.

"But I know what you are," the words tumbled out in a sing-song voice, and Cold Bear looked delighted to know this secret. "Why don't you face me in your other skin, and I will hang it in the trees, a tribute, so that all the forest will know, the mountains will know, that Bear is superior to Wolf."

"You are not worthy of my power," Amaoke told him, and was rewarded with a spiteful kick to the torso that broke several of his ribs.

Face me, coward," Cold Bear loosened the ropes at Amaoke's feet and untied his hands, then stood over him, mocking his weakened condition. His eyes widened somewhat when Amaoke accomplished the miracle of struggling to his feet.

Cold Bear waded in, ready to deliver more blows, but Amaoke doubted he could survive another such assault. Once the ropes slid off his wrists, he felt the *ulu* come to his hand, responding to a call he had not made, but he was grateful as always to feel its reassuring weight in his grip. He slashed through the air with it, meaning to gut his enemy.

But Cold Bear danced backward, out of reach, screaming in rage. "Face me! You will not fight me as a man! I am *aklark nigliktok,* the Cold Bear! Call your Wolf! It is beneath me to engage you while you are not all of yourself!"

Amaoke found this ironic since Cold Bear had already grievously injured him, and the man expected to win by his opponent's attrition.

"It would be unfair to you. You would be at a disadvantage against the Wolf, no matter that you walk in Bear's skin," Amaoke said calmly, although he was weakening and swayed with the effort it took to keep himself on his feet.

"Disadvantage?!" Cold Bear scoffed. "It is you who is overmatched. I smell your death upon you already. Make it a good death. Reach for it and I shall not prolong it."

Still Amaoke waited, as patient as he could afford to be. There was not much time, and he could not sustain another injury and expect to prevail. He stood still, knowing that in his rage and frustration Cold Bear would attack, and he was rewarded shortly. The man could not resist another taunt, but he miscalculated Amaoke's preternatural speed, and the *ulu* found flesh, spilling intestines into the snow.

Cold Bear looked surprised, and suddenly, Amaoke identified his scent among his innumerable memories. A small boy, cowering beside a tyrant father, crossing the river following the senseless murder of a wolf. And then he knew it all. That gentle boy had been groomed, tortured, broken, a monster engineered by the madman who begat him.

Cold Bear collapsed on the trail, in the middle of the snowy wood, and thirty years melted away. He smiled a little, and he knew that he should have done this very thing on that long-lost day. This was not so bad.

Amaoke watched the change in Cold Bear's eyes as the madness slipped away, replaced by the same lost, hurting expression he had seen on him as a boy. Amaoke felt the same protective, futile pity he had then, and knelt down next to him.

"*Aata?*" Cold Bear whispered, thinking he had never been so cold.

"No," Amaoke replied, settling close beside him on the path, unmindful of the bloody snow and his own many hurts, indeed, leaning in so the boy that was trapped within the man could hear him. "He cannot hurt you anymore."

Cold Bear nodded, and grateful to be free of the encumbrance of this life, he crossed the river of tears and was finally, mercifully, at peace.

innocence

bluestone lake
pipestem, west virginia
2013

"…in tonight's leading story, twenty-three schoolchildren between the ages of five and eleven disappeared today on their bus ride home. Authorities are suggesting that one of the buses that arrived to pick up the children at the end of the school day at Swallow Hills Elementary was a decoy. It appears to have been driven by an unknown suspect who allegedly abducted the children. So far, the Summers County Sheriff's office has no clear leads in this disturbing and distressing incident. According to witnesses at the school, the bus had markings that matched those from the Summers County School District fleet, although Director of Transportation Ryan Coombs reported to authorities that all of his vehicles are accounted for…"

1

WESTON REACHED THE CHURCH AT seven in the morning, saw its deserted appearance, and turned the old Buick around, heading back toward the highway to look for some breakfast. Although he had driven overnight, up through Tuscaloosa, Birmingham, and Knoxville, understanding the urgency of his task, he knew the local priest was probably still asleep in the rectory. Getting so little sleep himself, whether for a last-minute trip or not, Weston could not bring himself to deprive another of such a luxury. Another hour or two would not be too long, he hoped.

If the locals in the mom-and-pop diner gave the tall, bespectacled youth in the flowing cassock second glances, it was as much for his being a stranger as a priest, and perhaps his hippie-ish hair. When the waitress heard his soft bayou drawl, she was pleased he was a Southerner as well, although she did not really need that reason to like him. Not with a face like that. She looked at his collar and sighed. It figured; one way or another, the desirable ones were taken.

His familiars picked up on the local gossip, which was understandably focused on one thing. There was anguish, and some anger, and these emotions were unduly interesting to the demons. He paid attention only long enough to discern that none there had any useful information, there were none in that company that concealed knowledge related to the tragedy.

He finished his coffee and his eggs, trying, not for the first time, to fend off sleep deprivation with caffeine and fats. He tipped the waitress, and could not help blushing at her flirting, then pushed out the door with every eye in the place watching him.

On his return to the church, there were new signs of activity. A groundsman was out front, maneuvering a riding lawnmower skillfully around the church marquee. The smell of cut grass made Weston think of his grandfather. He noticed that the side door to the sacristy stood open. It was already getting warm, warmer than he had expected it would be this far north in mid-autumn, and he suspected that leaving the door ajar allowed for the cross breeze to circulate air.

He knocked at the door and stepped inside, hearing movement farther on, in the sanctuary. He found Father Ovedale redistributing prayer books. The overwhelming energy of the other priest's terror assaulted his senses, and he also read despair from him.

"Father Weston?" the man asked, nodding as if to answer his own question, and suddenly there was also relief in his expression.

"God be with you, Father Ovedale," Weston said, pulling the older man into his embrace, feeling sad about how frail he seemed, trying to calm his trembling.

"And also with you," the other priest replied. "I was just about to make tea," he added. "Would you like some?"

Weston nodded, thinking tea was probably just what was needed. It appeared that Father Ovedale had already had wine this morning, so perhaps his shakes were from more than fear.

They walked together to the kitchen, and Weston linked arms with him to try and provide some comfort and some calm. His own peace was shattered, because the demons sensed chaos here, and they fed from this man's dread.

Weston urged him to sit, and went to the stove, filling the teapot at the sink and setting it to boil. Church kitchens were all pretty much the same, there seemed to be a formula, and he made himself at home.

"Did you speak to the Archbishop?" Father Ovedale asked, as Weston was rattling through cabinets searching for teabags. The variation in the location of supplies was understandable; every church secretary had her own distinct sense of how things should be ordered. The one here was short, he decided, since the teabags were on the lowest shelf, making them slightly more difficult for him to see from his perspective, but easy for her to reach when she needed them.

"I received information from my own superiors," Weston told him. "But I always prefer the perspective of the local priest. This involves one of your parishioners, I am to understand, and you know them best."

Nothing more was said until the tea was ready, and they sat together for a moment in silence. Weston took the older priest's hand in his and prayed.

"Lord, give us the strength to face the enemy who threatens our faith in this world. Show us that it is your power that commands us, flows through us, and will provide victory over all evil we encounter. Comfort Father Ovedale in this time of hardship; stay with him as he takes this walk with me through the darkest of valleys. Help us trust in you as we should, and have the fortitude to make the sacrifices that are necessary to lead your children from this darkness."

When he finished praying, Father Ovedale did not release his hand. "Thank you for that, Father Weston. I have to admit that I have been struggling of late."

"It is understandable. So do we all. And fear can have great power over our hearts, it feeds on our doubt. Try to unburden yourself; it is no weakness to let God take it from you. Let Him succor your hurts." Weston squeezed his hand gently.

He could see that Father Ovedale's faith was faltering. He was being challenged by something he had never encountered before. This sort of event rarely occurred in everyday liturgical life; most priests did not have to face the inadequacies of their beliefs in the course of their careers.

"Now," Weston took off his spectacles and turned his attention to Father Ovedale. It made him appear more vulnerable, somehow, as was common in most people who wear eyeglasses, and he found that the gesture at times made those who were distressed better able to share their woes with him. "Please tell me why you alerted the Archbishop yesterday."

"You must understand, when those children disappeared, I just had a feeling…I-I…" Here, the priest stopped, his eyes moving about, and he blinked back tears rapidly. Weston pulled a napkin from the dispenser on the table and passed it to him. Ovedale took a deep breath and began again more slowly.

"This is a peaceful town. Nothing serious ever happens here. People leave doors unlocked. Neighbors help neighbors." He realized that he was putting something off, and corrected his course. "I don't know where the children are. Truly I don't. This is all my conjecture, come to because I have no other conclusion, and I cannot ignore my suspicions."

2

"YOU SEE, I HAVE A parishioner named Ernestine Brunelle. She originally moved up here from somewhere down South, Mississippi, perhaps, or Alabama? Somewhere coastal, near the Delta. She was a teacher and she taught for many years in the local schools. She would play the organ for us whenever our regular organist was out, she volunteered, she was continually active in the church. Certainly well-loved here in town.

"Her husband, Henry, was the light of her life. They had married young, and when it was discovered that they could not have children, he encouraged her to go to teacher's college, because she loved young people. That she could not bear her husband's children was the heartbreak of her life.

"They have been here going on forty years, much longer than I. When I was assigned to this parish I inherited their goodwill and witnessed the fruits of their many charitable works. Ernestine, especially, was a blessing. But she would rally Henry behind her, and they were quite invested in our little community. Every priest hopes for such a parishioner."

Weston nodded, waiting for the tragedy that he felt must be coming. He said nothing, just sipped his tea and waited for Father Ovedale to continue.

"Last spring, Henry took ill. It was tragic, really, they had both recently retired, and I know they were looking forward to the time together, and they had plans to travel and enjoy themselves." He stared off into some indeterminate place of memory for a moment, as if choosing his words. "It just came out of the blue. No one could find what was wrong with him. She took him to doctors in Charleston and Huntington, but nothing helped. He just wasted away, as though his life was being slowly leached from his bones.

"After he died, Ernestine disappeared. She stopped coming to church, and I understood that perhaps she was angry and grieving, so I let it be for a week or two. I tried to call out to the house, but got no answer, so I started to worry.

"I finally drove out to visit, kind of a cross between a welfare check and a reminder that she was loved. That I valued her as a part of our parish family, and wanted to bring her comfort if I could.

"The Ernestine I found that day was…simply wrong. I could see her face, hear her voice, but it was as if she had been replaced. She heard me pull up, and called to me from the back porch, but when I got there, I did not know what to think.

"Her mannerisms, her dress, her personality had all shifted. She was barely civil, as though she was tiptoeing on the edge of causing insult, and she protested any need for my help. When I offered to pray with her, she laughed.

"And it was at that moment, when she reflexively refused the comfort of prayer, that the back door of the house popped open, and a man emerged. He gave me such a start, as though my heart was growing in my chest, and I felt such a shrinking away from him that I thought in the moment I was taking ill.

"He was very striking, caramel skin and green eyes, handsome, but his very manner and expression were the complete opposite of the warm welcome I had always felt from Henry. I wondered if he were a relative come to help her after the funeral, but she rushed to introduce him.

"She said, suddenly just as sweet as you please, that she wanted to introduce her new man. She said his name was Jean St. Expédier, and that he was all the religion she needed, thank you very much. After that, it all seems so unclear, but what I can clearly recall is that they hurried me along to my car, they wanted me out."

Weston flinched when he heard the man's name, but Father Ovedale did not pick up on it, and kept talking.

"Truth is, I was so spooked and did not really know what to think. It was certainly her right to move on, but her beloved husband was not two weeks in his grave. And here she is sitting out on the back porch in her underslip, mooning over a man that had to be little more than half her age.

"Well, I was worried enough that I asked the county welfare office to check on her, because I wanted some official inquiry. I didn't want her to be stuck there with some con man taking advantage of her, even though she had seemed so smitten. What I reported was a suspicion of elder abuse."

"But they could not corroborate it," Weston guessed, and Father Ovedale smiled sadly.

"Worse than that," he replied. "She answered the door clean and groomed and told them that I was interfering. Didn't let them in the door, but held out her arm to the ordered living room as if to indicate she was managing fine. Asked them to tell me to let her be!"

"Trying to make your concern seem overreaching," Weston said, again squeezing Father Ovedale's hand.

"That's when strange things started happening," the old priest confided in a whisper, though they were alone, and the church was otherwise empty. "My secretary found a chicken heart on her desk one morning, dressed up with ribbon and bones to mimic the Sacred Heart icon. On another day, all my liturgies had been burned somehow, moved from where I had set them down in the sacristy to the altar.

"There were some desecrations outside the church, more mutilated chickens, occasionally just feathers and blood, once one nailed to the door of my office. The altar crucifix Jesus graffitied with blood tears. I got the sheriff involved, but the perpetrator was never caught.

"It doesn't feel safe here anymore," Father Ovedale admitted.

"I did not see Ernestine in town the whole summer," he continued. "It was so odd not to run into her at the post-office, or down at the firemen's breakfast. I was sad to have lost a friend.

"Then in September, I was doing my marketing up to the Kroger in Hinton, and there she was, picking through the produce right next to me. Well, it gave me a start.

"And though she was dressed as smartly as I had come to expect, her hair was not quite as neat, as though she had been doing it at home rather than coming into town. And she was still not the Ernestine I remembered.

"Other little things were off, her sandals were not fastened properly, the shoulder of her shift was askew. She had put a carton of eggs in her cart, but it was open, and one egg was missing.

"I greeted her and told her how pleased I was to run into her, but she just kept moving the tomatoes through her hands, picking one up, passing it from her right to her left hand, and then putting it back down. Then she repeated the process with another tomato, just over and over again, but she was not really looking at them.

"She said something that seemed odd at the time. Something like '*Jean and I are about to be blessed in the most wonderful way. And do you know he says that I can have my pick.*' She went on, but did not ever clarify what she was talking about.

"When I was just about to ask her for more details, I noticed a movement across from us, on the other side of the display. It was St. Expédier, staring at me with those cold eyes, and he was rolling that missing egg around in his fingers. And then he smiled at me, and held up the egg, and kissed it. It seems silly now, not much of anything, but it was one of the most frightening exchanges of my life. I knew he was threatening me. I was terrified. I left my groceries behind, nearly ran from the store. I know how it must sound."

Father Ovedale stopped, not, Weston thought, because the story was finished, but rather he needed to marshal his courage before telling the rest. He watched the older priest sip the now cold tea in front of him and waited.

After several quiet minutes, Father Ovedale extricated his hand from Weston's, putting it in his lap, clasping his hands together. His eyes were lost, but he began again, sounding slightly more resolute.

"Yesterday afternoon, when the children went missing, I was as shocked and astonished as anyone else, but had nothing to offer by way of help than my prayers." Abruptly he stood up, and so Weston did too, sliding his spectacles onto his face, sensing some new urgency. The terror was back.

"I should clear these cups," the older priest said, unnecessarily.

"Leave them," Weston touched his arm gently. "I will take care of it later."

Weston's touch seemed to give Father Ovedale courage, and he said quietly, "There is something…" And then his tears did come, and sobs of anguish, and he could speak no more.

Weston moved to embrace him, wanting to comfort him, but Father Ovedale evaded this attempt, shaking his head through his tears, and gestured for the other priest to follow him.

He led the way back, through the sanctuary, to a door at the opposite end from the sacristy. It opened onto a narrow staircase up to the second-floor rectory. Weston followed Father Ovedale to the landing, and then into the rectory bedroom.

It was warm and close in the heat, bright morning sunshine streamed into the room from two small windows that faced east. And beneath them, precisely arranged, lined up in a row along the wall, were twenty-three small shoes, the left of each pair they had once belonged to, a purposeful, ominous tableau.

Weston nodded resolutely, and said, "Have you notified the authorities?" He knew the diabolical seriousness of this finding. This knowledge the source of the older priest's anguish and terror. Not to mention that it could not be easily explained to county law enforcement, and it could easily incriminate this priest.

Father Ovedale shook his head mutely. "I found them when I came upstairs last night. I spoke with the Archbishop and exhorted him to believe me when I asked to report demonic influence as a factor in this kidnapping. I'm sure he thinks I am mad, but I told him it would be remiss for the Church to ignore it, and turn away from our duty to contribute to the return, the salvation of these children."

"He took you seriously," Weston said. "Did you tell him about the shoes?"

"N-no," Father Ovedale wept openly at this sin of omission. "I simply told him that one of my parishioners was in need of intervention. I finally understand. I should have seen it. Ernestine always wanted a child. She told me she would have her pick." He was almost gasping in horror, so Weston turned him away from that frightening display, steering him into the small adjacent sitting room and helping him settle in a chair.

Weston found the bathroom easily and filled one of the small paper cups from the dispenser next to the sink with cold water. This he handed to Father Ovedale, and asked for permission to use the telephone.

He dialed from memory, telling the international operator his code, doing some mental math about time zones, and smiling to himself. It was still daylight, there, one blessing.

Cardinal Mazuri answered the Pope's private line in Italian, so Weston spoke to him in that language.

"My work is confirmed," he said.

"The victim is Catholic?" Mazuri questioned.

"Yes. Devout. No known issues with baptism or confirmation. But tell His Holiness that it's a subset."

"Color?" Mazuri demanded impatiently.

"Violet," Weston replied, and waited on hold while his message was relayed. In lieu of hold music, he heard the words of the Pope's latest liturgical address. It was Cardinal Mazuri's way of expressing the passive-aggression he felt toward the young exorcist.

Soon, a familiar soothing voice came on the line.

"I need your permission to proceed," Weston said.

"You have it, my son. And my blessings. Be careful, and God be with you."

"Yes, Your Eminence, and also with you." Weston's next statement he made in code, for all that it sounded perfectly innocuous. He struggled with his moral compass for only a moment before adding, "I will need Public Relations on this one."

3

WESTON TURNED DOWN AN OILED dirt track that ran between two fields that had long since grown wild. The old Buick protested and groaned over the ruts. Still, his recent interventions to the aging suspension helped keep the car from bucking like a rodeo mount. He took his time, muttering prayers from Isaiah and Leviticus for comfort, feeling his own demons' frenzied anticipation as the car progressed toward the colonnaded house in the distance.

It was a grand structure, and perhaps at one time had been the pride of the county, but its outbuildings were now in poor repair, and the plantings were overgrown. Weston pulled up into the turnaround, and turned off the engine, listening, just listening, and after a bit, he could hear what he felt. Not the whisper of the wind through the trees, but voices, layered one atop the other, a confusion of sound, needling and insistent, like the drone of the cicadas. Except there were no cicadas. It was November.

The house should have been a cheerful affair, with its wraparound porches and white paint. But the upper windows were dark, and the air was still and heavy. Sorrow. He felt it immediately, as though it blanketed the place, had sunk deep into the soil. Death was here, too, and madness. It called to him. To the demons.

He curled his fingers around his rosary and prayed, as he did each time he had to face them anew, prayed for the strength, one more time, to face the unknown.

He got out of the car and looked around. His footsteps crunched over the pea-gravel path that had been laid down between the dirt drive and the house, curving one direction to the front door, and curving away opposite toward the rear of the house. Weston glanced speculatively toward the front porch, but turned toward the back, following the second path beneath a shady portico, with a trellis for ivy. It must have been lovely in the summer months, but the plantings looked dusty, neglected, perhaps dead.

The path took him to the porch that ran along the back of the house. It was a screened affair that overlooked a narrow finger of the lake at the bottom of the rear yard. He knew that his noisy steps announced him, but there was no immediate response from within.

Flies congregated inside the side door at the top of the steps, crawling over the screen with determined industry, their abbreviated bursts of flight as they alighted and landed over and over made a maddening sound, as if the heat angered them somehow.

He climbed up, opening the door, but as he had expected, none of them flew outside. He shrugged, and let himself in, greeting the woman who rocked rhythmically in the rocking chair that faced the back door. "Hello, Ernestine."

She was a solid woman who had to be in her sixties, but looked ten years younger. She was beautiful, with eyes the color of cognac that were set off to advantage against her chocolate skin. She wore only a thin chemise, and her curly hair corkscrewed out from her face in disarray. It looked like it hadn't been combed in a minute, as his Momma used to say.

She had a large bowl trapped between her knees, and she was calmly shelling peas as the flies buzzed around her head, a cloudy halo around a dark saint.

"Well, well, the Dark Man cometh," she replied, her voice whisky-rough with syrup at the end, a natural gift, since he doubted she had imbibed a drop of alcohol in her life or used a flake of tobacco. "It is truly an honor to have Papa Legba darken our door. Jean will be pleased."

He had no idea what she saw when she looked at him, but he knew all too well just who he looked like. The Morningstar. Ignoring this for the moment, he asked, "And where is Monsieur St. Expédier this fine morning?"

She smiled, peering at him from under her lashes. "Oh, he's here and there. But you and I, we're all alone for now. You're pret-ty, come closer and let Mama see you."

"*Ernesti-ine?*" Weston stretched the question out to get her attention, ignoring her request. "Where did you put those children?"

She stretched like a cat, one hand sliding over her breasts suggestively. "Oh, Mama knows," she crooned, and Weston's forehead wrinkled because now she was speaking to his demons. "I know how much all of you want to show him the pleasures of this world. Come to me, and I will give you my sweetness; I can help you crossover," she offered. Then she spoke again. This time directly to Weston. "Come to me, dear Prince. I promise I'll let you lick the bowl." She laughed when he flushed at this explicit invitation.

But he refused to be distracted, and he dropped the rosary from his palm, holding it out, letting the Cross and the Virgin dangle from his fingers. Her head snapped around, her eyes darting to it, twinkling like the dead dark gaze of a snake.

"Ernestine. Evangeline. Facilier. Brunelle." Weston said her true name one word at a time, seeing her surprise that she could not hide it from him, or rather, from his familiars. As each word fell from his lips, she writhed as if burned, or stung, by some noxious stimulus. "Where, I ask you? *For they are a heritage from the Lord, the fruit of the womb a reward.*" He quoted Psalm 127 to her, oddly sure that underneath, somewhere inside this lost woman, it would find its mark.

His words did seem to hurt her, and she paused, and looked confused, perhaps he had found the *real* Ernestine under the artifice. She shook her head from side to side, rolling it on her shoulders, and she began to shake and screech, her peas scattering as she dropped the bowl, and they bounced and rolled toward him like tiny accusations.

"They are unimportant," she straightened up suddenly, tilting her head in anger, moving to her next weapon since her sexuality had not served. "These kids will just grow up to cause more problems than they solve…teenage mothers, absent fathers…"

"But what about *your* life's work, Ernestine? The power of education?" Weston asked, watching her falter when he reminded her of her vocation. "Imagine the grief that this has caused. Think of those parents, young and afraid themselves. Don't you think that these youngsters aren't already disadvantaged enough in the eyes of this world? Innocence lost finds cynicism in the exchange."

"Who cares," she hissed, trying to dismiss this with a wave of her hand. Not before he saw her pause, and lose a step in her argument. His words were reaching their target.

"A waste," she hissed, with the lisping sibilance of a snake. "This place is not going to save them. West Virginia performs in the bottom fifty percent of public schools in the nation, this county lower than that. It cannot be helped. They will fuel something greater, be a part of something *transformative*." The last word was breathed out with reverent dreaminess.

Weston felt some measure of relief. Ernestine still fought, beneath it all, even if she were unaware, she still reasoned.

So he continued, "You will betray this abomination and reveal the secret. *Out of the mouths of babies and infants, you have established strength because of your foes, to still the enemy and the avenger.*" Psalms again, because he knew he was getting to her, speaking to the heart of the good woman's soul he had come to save, reminding her about the young lives that were at stake.

He beseeched her again, saying, "Ernestine, you must turn against this evil. Like a child does, you must sing the Lord's praises and spread his teaching with a glad, unfearing heart. To do so is to defeat the enemy, the one who shows us how to sin."

"I will show *you* how to sin," she replied, the temptress once more, though not before he saw a moment's sadness there. He decided not to answer, reserving himself for their next exchange, and let himself out the side door, saying only, "Get dressed, Ernestine. I'll be back shortly, and next time I am coming through the front door."

4

WESTON TOOK HIS TIME OUTSIDE, searching the grounds for any clue he could find. The outbuildings were quiet, too quiet, he thought. His familiars would often respond to any disturbance nearby. He was certain that the collective distress of twenty-three schoolchildren would call to them, but the demons were quiet, or rather, seemed more interested in the inhabitants of the main house.

Still, he was careful, and thorough. None of the accessory structures on the property seemed to have been accessed recently, the dried vegetation evidence of robust seasonal growth over the summer without intervention from any gardening effort or trimming during the autumn. Their windows were dark and dirty, cobwebbed, abandoned by the spiders and other insects by this time of the year.

He quartered the yard, and foraged in both fields flanking the drive, indeed, walked all the way back to the road. He checked the mailbox, but it was empty. The grassy tufts beneath it were as neglected as the rest of the garden.

He walked the waterline, and peered carefully at the underside of the dock. He followed the footprint of the house, checking under the porches as well, examining the crawl spaces behind the dormant hedges, allowing his righteous anger to return.

He went to the car and retrieved a few of his usual tools, and one extremely specific additional item. An ounce of prevention. This he placed around his neck, tucking out of site beneath his cassock.

He climbed the front porch steps with deliberation, allowing his heavy tread to announce his return. Between the top of the steps and the front door, there was a line of white powdery material. He smeared a bit of it with the toe of his Converse and smiled. Chalk dust and salt.

Weston crossed the line and rapped firmly on the screen door. The heavy front door stood open, and he could see into the shady interior. There was no immediate movement that he could see, so he knocked heavily again.

In a moment, Ernestine swept into the room, with no small amount of exaggeration. She wore an old-fashioned cocktail dress, like a debutante, with a stiff starched crinoline under the skirt. There was a pearl choker with some sort of elaborate pendant at her throat, and when she reached the door she put her hand on her chest with a dramatic gesture of surprise.

She wore no shoes, and her hair had not been touched. From the neck down, save for her bare feet, of course, she was oddly June Cleaver-ish. It gave Weston the creeps.

"Prince Charming," she swooned and simpered.

"Ernestine Evangeline Facilier Brunelle, let me in." Weston tried to sound bored and set aside his anger and impatience.

She merely gave him an arch look out of the side of her eye.

"Please," he added, genuinely.

She nodded, and backed away from the screen, but did not open the door herself, which he found interesting, if unsurprising. Her faith had bound her in this prison. Faith and latent superstition. In the Bayou and along the Delta were many people who blended tenets of

Christianity with a West African faith that was much older, a syncretism that Weston felt was contributing heavily to his labors in this house.

Weston had no trouble with the door, and if she had thought he would have trouble crossing the threshold, she was mistaken. The surprise was written on her face.

"Have you been messing with the Shadow Man, Ernestine?" Weston asked, and she ducked her head, not wanting to answer him.

"I need, I want, I need, I want – why, I want to get the tea," she stuttered, finally recovering her poise with a slow turn of her head, remembering to be a good hostess. "I have all but forgotten my manners!" She said this last in a sing-song voice as she retreated to the kitchen, leaving him alone once more.

But she popped right back out through the doorway like a scary, sneaky Jack-in-the-Box, carrying a tray with a china teapot and flowered cups and saucers.

"Here we are!" she trilled, setting her burden on the sideboard, and inviting Weston to sit. He shook his head, but accepted the cup and saucer she offered after she had poured out. "Milk? Sugar?" she offered sweetly, her eyes watching him, sharp like a predatory raptor's.

He sniffed the steam rising from the cup. Sulfur, and a trace of something else – honey – which she had mistakenly thought might disguise it.

He set it aside, expertly balancing the cup on the saucer as he returned it to the tray. "I don't suppose you have any jimson weed," he couldn't resist saying, part in earnest, and part out of that awkward need he had to joke when he was nervous. Ernestine paused, as if stuck, searching the internal script for a response.

But Weston turned away from her, and took another approach, calling out to the depths of the house. "Bayou John! Show yourself!"

He leaned toward the stairway and looked up. Ernestine moved to keep herself in front of him, block his path. Her face was a mask of anger and distress.

"Whom are you calling for?" she tried to disclaim in a voice that suggested no one else was there.

"Jean St. Expédier, your paramour," Weston spat out the name and watched her recoil just as certainly as if he had struck her. "Saint Expedite, so named for his ability to quickly prepare souls for the farewell passage. The Death Bringer, eater of pureflesh, right hand of the Lord of the Flies."

Ernestine's eyes grew large, and she shook her head from side to side, faster and faster. "No, you mustn't. I cannot betray him."

"ERNESTINE." Weston's voice became a command that seemed to fill the house. "You are a child of God, and you must renounce this evil. *Thou shalt not steal*, you may *not* pick a stolen child to hold to your breast. *Thou shalt not kill*, you may *not* abandon the others to their deaths. You will heed the words of the prophet Isaiah. *All your children shall be taught by the Lord, and great shall be the peace of your children*."

Tears flowed from Ernestine's eyes and her body trembled, as if she were having a seizure, but she closed her mouth, apparently determined in her course. She turned hateful eyes upon Weston and shook her head. "He loves me," she hissed through gritted teeth, hyperventilating with the effort of her resistance to these sacred words.

And then the energy in the room changed, and his familiars were excited, and Weston felt the pull of the pseudologues, flowing over and around his skin. He turned to find a man standing beside him, his age about thirty years, his brassy complexion and bright emerald eyes betraying his Creole background. But despite the unfamiliarity of his countenance, Weston knew he had given his flesh to the Death Bringer, who was manipulating him.

The man reached for him, but Weston tugged on the small item he had placed around his neck, letting it fall outside his cassock and rest against his chest.

St. Expédier stared at it in horror, pulling his hands away. "The *gris-gris!*" he shuddered, stumbling and twisting backward.

"Yes, my friend," Weston agreed. "A little gift from *my* friend, Priestess Miriam, in the Quarter.

"You see, I play chess with her once a month. It's part of my interfaith outreach, to show my respect to other religious leaders in the community.

"She doesn't take kindly to the subversion of her faith, nor does she tolerate the abuse of Papa Midnite's power. She gave this to me once, worried about my safety, I guess. I suppose I *do* experience the occasional occupational hazard," Weston mused. In another voice, holding out the Redeemer Cross, he said, "Out, *Asmodeus,* for this house is a sacred place, inhabited by those who love the Lord."

The china in the cabinet on the far wall rattled as the pseudologues responded to the Death Bringer's fury and were compelled to flee from the divine talisman. Weston heard the bang of the screen door, and turned to see St. Expédier sprinting away from the house.

Weston let him go, unworried about this development, and turned back to Ernestine as he felt the pseudologues slide over him and away, following *le grande zombi*.

Ernestine was pale, and unmoving, and he realized that she was in danger. If St. Expédier had followed the rituals, and brought her through the stages of preparation and invocation, and ultimately into this possession, now, because Weston had disrupted his influence, Ernestine could progress to farewell, casting off the demonic control along with her life.

Weston concentrated. There was something he was supposed to be remembering, and it was at the periphery of his thoughts. Something from his scholarship, something he knew that Miriam had taught him.

At that moment, Ernestine saved him, because she reached absentmindedly for her throat. *Of course*, he thought, looking more closely at the pendant on her necklace.

He reached out and captured it in his strong fingers and squeezed. The thin shell of this *ouanga* broke under his efforts, and ashes and fingernail clippings fell onto his palm. It felt like a living thing, and he flinched but curled his hand around the contents.

Ernestine gave a soft cry, like relief, and fainted away. He knelt over her and listened to her heart, which was strong and steady. She breathed restfully, and he was satisfied she would survive.

He reached into the pocket of his cassock, and anointed her with sacred oil, making the sign of the cross with it on her forehead. He placed his rosary gently around her neck.

He got back to his feet, and whispered a prayer of hopefulness, calling on Christ to help this poor priest find the lambs before it was too late.

5

HE DAWDLED IN THE PARLOR, looking at the many things that Ernestine and her husband had saved, reading a story of their lives, trying to gain some better understanding of them, looking for anything that might help him now.

In the china cabinet was a small figurine, on closer inspection it was a tiny bride and groom, their wedding cake topper, but it appeared to be damaged. In particular, there was a crack and a chip out of the center of the groom, the porcelain marred. It was subtle, and understandably could have been broken at any time during their years together, but he suspected that this small defect was related to poor Henry's demise, the way that the *vodun* magic had been initiated. It saddened him, but he could not linger over this, aware every second of the urgency of his errand.

His eye caught on something colorful in the parlor beyond the stairs, and he walked toward it. A collection of handmade dolls, appropriate to a woman who had always yearned for children.

Each tiny face was lovingly painted on the dark walnut head of an old-fashioned wooden clothespin. Miniature black curls had been painstakingly drawn over the tops, and the monotony of their faces had been broken up by the artist's use of a variety of types of colored cloth glued to the shafts for clothing.

As Weston approached, something about this symmetry bothered his brain, and he counted them. In astonishment, he counted again.

There were twenty-three of them, exactly twenty-three, and his skin felt cold.

He put his face down near them and looked even more closely. All the colors on the clothing were too bright and modern to be aged calico or hand-dyed muslin. Then his eye caught an incongruous pattern, grey-green on orange, and he realized he was seeing part of a screen-printed dinosaur.

He gasped. The scraps of clothing glued to the wooden pins had been taken from the children. He opened his hand and softly blew the ashes from the poisonous charm he had destroyed over the tiny dolls. And just like that, the spell was broken.

He could faintly hear the weak cries of many little voices coming from somewhere on the property, his demons excitable and drawn to the sound. Weston gripped the Redeemer Cross tightly in his hand and ran for the door.

It took him a moment to get his bearings in the yard, and now that the magic was broken, he realized his mistake, was able to see what the spell had hidden. There was a door to one of the outbuildings facing the lake that had been recently used, and he put his shoulder to the old wood and broke it down, following the sounds of fearful distress from inside.

"We're here! Please let us out!" one of the children cried, and Weston inched forward in the gloom, letting his eyes adjust, navigating in the waning afternoon sunshine.

The building was one of the largest on the property, and what he found was astonishing and heartbreaking. All of the children, none older than eleven or twelve, and a few little more than toddlers, stood at the bottom of a nine-foot water reservoir.

There must have been an underground pipe that connected the tank to the lake, since there were at least three and a half feet of water in the bottom. It was too deep for them to sit down, indeed he could see that some of the older children had linked their arms together to help keep the younger ones afloat, and it was clear that they were reaching the end of a terrifying and exhausting struggle to keep standing or drown.

He quickly pulled his cassock open, popping the buttons in his haste, and removed it, shrugging it off over his head. He kneeled on the wet, mossy stones, feeling the moisture soak through his pantlegs in an instant, but did not pause, lying down on his belly, ignorant of the mess it made of his clothes.

Using the benefit of his long reach, he lowered the garment to the water, and the tallest of the children tugged it doubtfully, so Weston said, "I'm here now, you're safe, I promise I will get you out. If you can, bring the smaller kids first, and try to lift them up a bit."

The boy did better than that. He enlisted the girl next to him, who looked to be about his age, and the two of them, with no minor struggle and ignoring their own exhaustion, assisted the smaller children to get onto their shoulders and stand.

From such a perch, Weston could get ahold of their forearms, and one by one he pulled each of them to safety. When the oldest were the last two remaining in the tank, they looked at one another, both spent, panting and shaking.

Weston said, "Just a bit more. Concentrate for a bit more. Taking the neck of the cassock in one hand, and the hem in the other, he lowered this like a sling. And seeing the rolling whites of their eyes, their fear of being the last one alone in the pit, he said, "Both of you. Come together. Stand with your back to the side of the tank. Put your arms and head through the loop. Keep your hands tight against your sides and don't give up. I'm going to slide you up against the wall. I'll do all the work. Just hold on."

Not for the first time, but certainly for the best one, he was grateful for all his hours on the weight bench. He managed to get them to the lip of the tank, but it was slippery and afforded them no purchase. On his belly he could lift them no farther.

"You'll have to grab my shirt, and climb up over my head," Weston told them. "Each of you take a side so I can help you."

In their flailing, scrambled panic to escape their prison, his spectacles came off, tumbling end over end into the pool below, where they were swallowed with a soft splash.

"Oh, I'm so sorry," said the girl, whose final push had liberated his glasses.

"Don't worry," he gently ran a finger along her cheek, and smiled in reassurance. "I'd rather have you guys."

And he huddled with them there, and caught his breath, reaching out long arms to pull them all close, his fingers curling into their clothing, feeling their curls against his face, and clutching them tightly. They clung to him as he got slowly to his feet, and not one of them let go as he led them back to the house to call 911.

They were cold, and wet, each missing one shoe, and they limped on feet macerated and broken from the water. They had survived nearly twenty-seven hours in that hell.

When the firetruck and the county ambulances arrived, they were all still clutching whatever part of him they could hold. And they refused to release him until each of their parents arrived, when they were assured of a new safety from the old.

Ernestine responded to smelling salts, and she was transported for evaluation and any treatment she might need. Mercifully, she seemed to be ignorant of the events of much of her recent captivity.

Weston made his statement to the county and state authorities, providing a description of St. Expédier, knowing it was unlikely he would ever be found. Weston thought that the name was likely an alias, and he suspected the man to be a known practitioner of voodoo, who may have fled his home out of fear of reprisal for some other evil mischief. Perhaps whatever dark arts he had dabbled in had been what had brought him to the attention of the Death Bringer. It sounded like the authorities had already uncovered a bit of information that might help connect St. Expédier to the case, and possibly allow them to close it.

Weston emphasized his strong opinion that Ernestine had been ignorant of these crimes. He told the sheriff that he felt she had been poorly used, and taken advantage of by a con man who had preyed on her in her grief following the death of her husband. The sheriff seemed to know Ernestine well already, seemed to be genuinely concerned about her well-being.

Once that was done, he walked through to the screen porch and sat in one of the rocking chairs, looking out at the dark void of the lake. When finally he stopped shaking, he stood up and let himself out the side door he had first used to enter the house earlier that day.

A furtive movement in the yard caught his attention, and he walked in the direction of the tree line. The Death-Bringer, still wearing its stolen skin, looked out at him through St. Expédier's eyes.

"There were so many of them," it shook its head. "You know you're one of us. You could have at least let me have one of those delicious children."

Weston gripped the Redeemer Cross firmly in his right hand and connected a righteous blow to the demon's face, and St. Expédier was no more, exploding into a cloud of dust as fine as talc.

And as his demons rose up in satisfaction at this act of angry vengeance, he heard the Serpent's voice in his mind. *You really need to work on your sense of humor, Chosen One.*

6

THE LOST SHOES WERE NEVER found.

They were not in the house, or any of the outbuildings, or on the grounds of the property. Police dogs were brought in to search to no avail. The children understandably did not remember what had happened to their footwear.

The West Virginia Bureau of Investigation even got county budget approval to drag the lake. Their divers examined the outflow pipe coming from the tank and vacuumed the sludgy bottom beneath the pier.

Jean St. Expédier eluded them as well. But to a person, every one of the authorities that had worked on the problem agreed, that the worst thing about the whole case was the unsolved mystery of those missing left shoes.

The Archdiocese of New Orleans received a package with a Hinton, West Virginia, postmark in December, around the time one might normally expect a Nativity gift.

The item inside was removed, cleaned, and returned to its owner.

Author's Note

These stories were written in May 2020, when we were largely still sheltering from the COVID-19 pandemic, still in quarantine, during a time of great economic, social, and racial unrest.

May is traditionally short-story month, and I had a few fragments of ideas for the NSEW characters. These are windows into their lives that had nothing to do with the arc of the novels, and so they had been in that strange purgatory for stories that exists in every writer's brain. From that place, they wheedle and cajole, demons that only get angrier with time, howling to be set free. As most of you know, my sanity is both questionable and tenuous, so needs must get them out.

Additionally, because at least one of these stories could have become an unwieldy beast (a rare and truly supernatural creature called a novella) with a forty-thousand-word count, I put some restraints on the exercise. I restricted myself to a maximum of six chapters (arbitrary) for each story with the goal to create unity among them. I addressed using concept titles, or themes. The final challenge was to have the title appear within the text of each one.

But as often happens, art imitates life, the events of the world around me influenced the direction of the fairy tales, and I found myself emphasizing the humanity, love, and redemption that exists in each one of these small escapes. Each story focuses on the crucial question, *who decides the value of a human life?* Whether on the basis of spurious social status, skin color (or lack thereof), mental illness compounded by the xenophobic cruelty of paternalistic colonialization, or a perceived lack of future potential.

In this short compilation, I have visited old friends without overstaying my welcome, and I hope you enjoyed seeing them again as well.

About the Author

LJ Farrow is a Colorado native who now lives and writes in rural Indiana.

www.ingramcontent.com/pod-product-compliance
Lightning Source LLC
Chambersburg PA
CBHW070908160726
48004CB00003B/1280